"I hope I didn't frighten them too much."

Cash crouched beside the box and ran the tips of his fingers across the kittens' soft fur. "I suspect the mama cat is going to be the most difficult to deal with." He flashed the back of his left hand. Angry red claw marks etched the skin.

"Your poor hand," Alyssa murmured sympathetically. "Between the cat and your hammer..." She was serious, but she added a teasing note in her voice.

"Rub it in, why don't you?"

She chuckled. "Can I help it if you're a walking accident just waiting to happen?" *Who also happens to save kittens.*

He snorted. "That about sums it up."

Their gazes met and locked for a moment before she looked away.

Her heart was rapidly beating, and she took a deep breath, concentrating on slowing her pulse to its normal rate.

She tried to tell herself that it was just the adrenaline of having found the litter of kittens, but deep inside, she knew better...

A *Publishers Weekly* bestselling and award-winning author with over 1.5 million books in print, **Deb Kastner** writes stories of faith, family and community in a small-town Western setting. She lives in Colorado with her husband and a pack of miscreant mutts, and is blessed with three daughters and two grandchildren. She enjoys spoiling her grandkids, movies, music (The Texas Tenors!), singing in the church choir and exploring Colorado on horseback.

Visit the Author Profile page at Harlequin.com for more titles.

A Christmas Baby
for the Cowboy

Deb Kastner

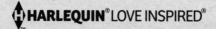

HARLEQUIN® LOVE INSPIRED®

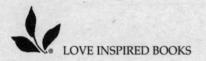

LOVE INSPIRED BOOKS

Recycling programs
for this product may
not exist in your area.

ISBN-13: 978-1-335-50992-5

A Christmas Baby for the Cowboy

www.Harlequin.com

Printed in U.S.A.

Seek ye the Lord while he may be found, call ye upon him while he is near: Let the wicked forsake his way, and the unrighteous man his thoughts: and let him return unto the Lord, and he will have mercy upon him; and to our God, for he will abundantly pardon.
—*Isaiah* 55:6–7

To the choir
at St. John the Baptist Catholic Church.
You are my tribe and I'm incredibly blessed to
be a part of this wonderful, talented group.

Chapter One

"Cash Coble, front and center, please."

Jo Spencer, the bubbly elderly redhead serving as the auctioneer, had more energy in her pinky finger than Cash had in his whole body, and her warbling voice made his head throb mercilessly.

Cash, a rodeo bareback rider only recently returned to his hometown of Serendipity, Texas, winced at the high-pitched feedback of the microphone that followed his name being called over the loudspeaker. The screechy whine drilled straight into the space between his eyes.

He was the next bachelor on the docket at Serendipity's First Annual Bachelors and Baskets Auction in the middle of June.

But if he had his way, he would be anywhere but here.

The last thing he wanted right now was to display himself for all his hometown to see. He'd left Serendipity in the dust when his rodeo career had taken off and he hadn't been home since—with good reason.

Now he had no choice. Even if he'd rather slink off to the nearest bar and drink himself into forgetfulness.

"Remember," said his publicist, Martin Brandt, stepping back a pace as he surveyed Cash from the tip of his boots to the top of his hat. "You get up there and turn on your cowboy charm. Don't forget to smile. I have a photographer from *Rodeo Times* here to document this, so you'd better make good out there if you want your career back."

Cowboy charm.

That was what had got him into this predicament in the first place. His once-handsome face and enormous ego.

He scoffed under his breath. There wasn't one blessed thing that could even remotely be considered *charmed* about his life right now.

What was the opposite of charmed, anyway?

Pete Drexler grinned and held up his camera as Martin leaned up on tiptoe and adjusted Cash's black cowboy hat, presumably to reveal more of his eyes. The middle-aged publicity agent was a diminutive fellow who stood no taller than five feet even. Cash, at six-one, towered over him.

But what Martin lacked for in size, he made up for in vigor, and he was one of the best agents in the business, with all the attitude of a T. rex in obtaining the best for his clients.

Cash hated being bossed around by the man. Sometimes he had to grit his teeth to fight from barking back, especially when he was feeling as physically out of sorts as he was right now. But Martin was the only one in the rodeo world who hadn't dumped him after all that had recently happened to him, and Cash appreciated his loyalty.

Cash's advertising sponsors had dropped him like a hot potato when his life had turned into a downward spiral after his best friend, Aaron Emerson, had died.

Martin could easily have done the same. Having Cash as a client couldn't be good for his reputation, and yet Martin had persisted, believing in Cash when he didn't even believe in himself. There was a lot to be said for that kind of commitment.

Martin had this inspired idea that Cash could prove himself worthy of advertising support and save his public image by participating in this bachelor auction, not only because his agent expected Cash to be popular with the ladies, but because it was for charity.

What better way to show that Cash was a changed man?

Cash didn't blame his sponsors for dropping him. Carrying a secret darker and thicker than tar affected every area of his life, from blackouts after nights of hard drinking to losing his stamina on the rodeo circuit.

He was a down-and-out, has-been cowboy, and deserving every bit of what was coming to him. Up to and including the ridicule and humiliation he would suffer as he stood on an auction block with little to no expectations of being bid on.

When he'd been a winner, nobody blamed him for his actions. Young cowboys were expected to let off steam. He got a pass.

But now?

Who would want him?

A big fat nobody. That's who.

Yet he had to try. Rodeo was the only thing left for him.

If he lost that, well…

He would lose everything.

The good folks in Serendipity had gotten together to raise funds for a new senior center and hospice. With such an outstanding cause, townsfolk had come out in droves and were opening their hearts and pocketbooks with cheerful generosity.

The bachelor auction, where a single man would offer his particular expertise and skill set to the winner, had originally been Jo's idea, but it hadn't taken long for married men to sign on, as well.

Did a young woman need her car fixed? Carpentry? Plumbing? Accounting? Painting? Laying hardwood flooring?

There was a man for that.

Refusing to be outdone, Serendipity's women had decided to chip in by preparing down home country meals served in festive picnic baskets to the men they bid on. All for a good cause and all in good fun.

He'd given up praying the night Aaron had died, but he mumbled under his breath something that might have been a prayer. He hoped this scheme of Martin's wouldn't backfire. Cash didn't know how it could get any worse, but with the downhill slide he was on, it wouldn't surprise him if it did.

He growled under his breath and climbed the stairs to the makeshift platform. He'd watched the previous bachelors hamming it up for the crowd, curling their biceps and showing off their muscles. One guy had even run up a tree and done backflips across the stage, much to the audience's amusement.

Cash was an athlete on the back of a horse, but he couldn't do a backflip to save his life. He wasn't going to flex his biceps, either, not even if Martin pressed him to do so. The auction was already degrading as it was. If the ladies wanted to bid on him, they would just have to take him as is.

He plucked off his hat, curling the brim in his fist until his knuckles hurt. The muscles in his shoulders and arms clenched, resisting the sudden hush of the crowd.

Instead of the cheering and catcalls the other men had received, people were either staring mutely or whispering to their neighbors behind their hands.

He glanced at Martin, who gestured for him to do something, but there was nothing to do. He'd made an entrance, all right, just not the kind he'd wanted.

Raising his chin, he gazed across the crowd. No one would meet his eyes.

His throat was as raw as sandpaper and he couldn't keep still. He wiped his free hand across the rough material of his jeans, stilling a tremor that had nothing to do with his snapping nerves at being plunked in front of an unyielding audience, and everything to do with counting the minutes since the last time he'd experienced the sweet burn of alcohol.

He was as dry as the Sahara. He'd thought that after three days, he ought to be over the worst of the physical withdrawal, but if anything, he was feeling worse now than he had those first horrible couple of days.

This—*abstention*—wasn't a part of his cleanup act—or at least not one meant for the benefit of the camera. Drying out was his own personal journey, made by his own choice and determination.

At the moment, it was his own personal torment.

"Now, ladies and gents," Jo announced in a sing-song voice, "you'll be happy to hear that our very own Cash Coble is back in town, fresh from his success on the national rodeo circuit."

Success?

That was embellishing the truth if Cash had ever heard it, but he appreciated Jo for trying to help him. A man was only successful until he wasn't.

And Cash *wasn't*.

"Now, anyone can see that Cash here is easy on the eyes. Better yet, his agent informs me that he is ready and willing to help you out, no matter how big or small your project. Whatever odd job you've got, Cash is your man, ladies."

This was usually the point where the crowd broke into an uproar of laughter and the single ladies started tossing out bids.

However, the entire crowd was acting peculiar, milling around in small groups and having personal conversations rather than paying attention to the unsteady cowboy rooted to the platform.

No one called out a bid.

Not. One. Woman.

While Serendipity was full of good people, Cash knew how easy it was for gossip to flood such a small town. A perpetual game of Telephone where the story changed bit by bit as it went from person to person.

Cast blame first and find out the truth later.

Only in Cash's case, the truth was far worse than anything these spectators' minds could conjure, something he would carry with him to his grave, a burden that was his alone to bear.

"Come on, ladies," Jo urged. "Let's see those hundred-dollar bills waving in the air. Remember, it's for a good cause," she reminded everyone. "The new senior center ain't going to build itself without your generosity, so I'm going to ask you again. Who will start the bidding at one hundred dollars?"

Cash waited, tapping his hat against his thigh.

Nothing.

There wasn't a single bid, even with Jo's urging. And if Jo couldn't get a response from this otherwise receptive crowd, there was no hope whatsoever for Cash.

People might not believe it from the way he'd been acting recently, but he had a heart, and it was stinging nearly as bad as his ego.

There was no way he would let anyone in Serendipity know how their collective rejection affected him. He shook his head and scoffed audibly, then straightened his shoulders, jammed his black Stetson on his head and turned to stomp down the platform stairs.

"Three hundred dollars," came a female voice that carried across the silence with the pure tone of a bell.

He turned to scan the crowd.

Who had bid on him?

"Once, twice, sold," Jo said, speaking faster than any real auctioneer Cash had ever heard. She banged her gavel on the podium that had been placed on the stage for just that purpose. "Alyssa Joan Emerson, come on up here and rope your prize."

Of all people, not only an Emerson, but Lizzie—*Alyssa*. He couldn't get over how his best friend's kid sister had bloomed into a beautiful woman. Her wavy strawberry-blond hair was grown out now, more blond than strawberry. He didn't recall her eyes being so very...*brown*, like deep, rich dark chocolate.

Little Lizzie Emerson, all grown up.

Alyssa wasn't in all that much of a hurry to claim her *prize*, as Jo had called winning Cash Coble. She wasn't sure she'd made the right decision at all. This might very well rank up there among some of the most foolish decisions she'd ever made.

But when no one else offered to buy Cash, her soft heart had gotten the best of her and her mouth had worked faster than her head.

Her oldest brother, Eddie, accused her of letting her empathy get the best of her. She led with her heart instead of her head. She felt too deeply—and then acted on those emotions even—*often*—to her own detriment.

She couldn't seem to help herself. She chose to believe the best about people, even when they showed themselves to be untrustworthy.

Was she crazy, bringing Cash back into her life? Even without all she'd heard about the kind of man he'd turned out to be, she suspected Cash would be a problem for her.

She had so many other challenges to face.

Despite her best efforts, tears burned at the backs of her eyes and she blinked rapidly. Cash would be a constant walking, talking reminder of the brother she had recently lost. Cash and Aaron had been best friends since childhood. After graduating from high school, they had traveled the pro rodeo circuit together.

Sweet, fun-loving Aaron.

How was it that he'd been the one to get behind the

wheel of a car drunk and fatally crash into a tree when Cash was still alive?

It didn't seem fair.

Alyssa was ashamed that such a horrible thought had passed through her mind, and yet there it was.

She didn't want Cash here. She wanted her big brother back, with his jokes and smiles and unceasing teasing.

Ironically, there had been a time when she would have given anything to have Cash notice her. As a teenager, Cash had worked in the Emerson family's hardware store part-time. Their store was the town catchall, not only carrying hardware, but boots, clothing, gardening supplies and animal feed. Once upon a time, she'd had a crush on the boy whose dark hair flopped over his forehead and into his impossibly blue eyes, but too much had happened in her life since high school to consider those errant feelings as anything more than childhood fantasies.

Little Lizzie Emerson had grown up. While she was still called Lizzie by a select few of her closest friends, most people now referred to her by her given name, Alyssa.

She didn't give much stock to rumors, but from what she'd heard around town, Cash was a heavy drinker. He'd got a woman pregnant and then walked away from his responsibilities to the baby. She couldn't respect a man like that.

She had no idea why she'd piped up with a bid at the last second.

Well, no, that wasn't entirely true. Cash was the logical man for the job she had in mind. He'd worked at Emerson's Hardware in his youth and already knew how she did things. She could put him straight to work without having to explain everything.

Which was why, despite everything, he was a good fit for the work she needed done. Kickfire, a major brand name in boots and Western wear, had contracted with her to sell their products in her store. That meant a lot of rearranging, building new display cases, creating a window display and, just before Black Friday, putting out the new stock.

But she wasn't really going to trust him. Emerson's was the one solid thing she had left in a world that had completely tilted awry.

She intended to lay down the rules and keep a sharp eye on Cash to make sure he didn't screw up.

But first things first. She threaded her way to the front of the crowd and marched up onto the stage. This auction was supposed to be fun, and she'd been looking forward to it for weeks. Count on her to make a cheerful town event into something stressful instead of something sweet.

Nice one, Alyssa.

"Here's your lariat, dear," Jo said, pressing the rope into her hand. "Now, you go lasso your handsome cowboy."

Cash wiped the sweat from his brow, then planted his hat back on his head, challenging her with his gaze.

Wonderful. He was intentionally making it more difficult for her to successfully swing a loop around him. She could adjust the lariat until it was big enough to go over Cash even with his hat on, but it wasn't as if she was an expert roper. She owned a hardware store. If her toss was the slightest bit off, the coil would bounce right off his black Stetson.

Was he throwing down the gauntlet? Did he think she wasn't good enough for him?

Tough bananas. She was the only one willing to rescue him today and he was just going to have to deal.

Was he expecting all the pretty single ladies to treat him as if he was still hot stuff, falling all over him as they'd done when he was a teenager?

Well, he wasn't.

Not anymore.

He most definitely wasn't a teenager. He'd filled out in all the right places. He'd grown a couple of inches taller. His shoulders were broader, his face a hard chisel of lines and his muscles more defined.

But for all that, he wasn't *hot stuff* anymore.

Now that she was closer to him, she could see that his eyes were sunken into his head, with dark circles shadowing his gaze. His skin was roughened from the sun, which might have appeared rugged were it not for the stress lines on his forehead and etched around his eyes. The week's worth of scruff on his face only increased the shadow.

"Do something, Cash," demanded a man in the crowd, a voice Alyssa couldn't identify.

Alyssa's gaze switched to a short man in a gray suit and shiny black shoes. Everyone else in the crowd had on blue jeans.

Alyssa looked back at Cash and raised an eyebrow in question.

"Let's get this over with, Lizzie." Cash swept his hat off his head with a grunt and gestured for her to rope him.

Alyssa adjusted the lariat and swung it in the air a couple of times to get a feel for the weight. She was a shopkeeper's daughter and had zero ranching experience, but she was standing all of two feet away from Cash.

How hard could it be?

She swung the rope toward Cash, mimicking the actions she'd seen her brother Eddie and her neighboring rancher friends do a thousand times. But instead of soaring in a nice loop up and around Cash, the noose tightened too early and swung off to one side.

It would have dropped to the ground, but at the last moment, Cash's hand darted out to grab it. Her cheeks heated as Cash slowly and deliberately loosened the lariat and threaded himself through it until the noose circled his waist.

Was he intentionally trying to embarrass her?

Well, she wasn't going to let him.

She yanked the rope tight around Cash and turned her back on him, leading him off the platform, her fashionable cowboy boots thumping loudly down the stairs. She didn't care when the rope became taut and he appeared to be pulling back, scuffling his feet behind her.

Too bad for him that she was more stubborn than he was. If he was going to dig in his heels, she would just pull harder. He'd have to give in sometime.

She was relieved when they were finally off the stage and could pause while Cash pulled the rope off from around himself, tossing it back to Jo for use with the next bachelor.

Now, at least, they could find somewhere semiprivate to talk—not that there was anywhere on the community green, already spotted with dozens of brightly decorated picnic baskets, that could be considered truly private.

She sighed deeply.

"Follow me," she said. "My picnic basket is over there, in the shade of that oak tree. I brought a lot of food. I hope you're hungry."

Cash muttered something unintelligible, but he stayed by her side as she led him to the basket she'd prepared. Thankfully, she'd arrived early at the community green, wanting to complete a last-minute check, since her family's store, Emerson's Hardware, had provided all the materials to make the platform.

It also allowed her to secure a prime spot on the lawn. The sun was shining brightly and there wasn't a cloud in the sky, so the shade would be welcome.

Of course, she'd made her little banquet with a cute single bachelor in mind. Never mind that she knew every available guy in town and had either already dated him or wasn't remotely interested in doing so.

One of the woes of a single woman growing up in a small town. She longed for the special connection that was somehow missing in the few boyfriends she'd had over the years.

Not that it really mattered. After everything that had happened recently, she had neither the time nor the energy to pursue a romantic relationship.

It was all she could do to keep her head above water, between the hardware store renovation and struggling to keep the business afloat virtually on her own.

Recently, she'd also begun to make all sorts of changes according to the contract she'd signed with Kickfire.

Eddie had abandoned the shop for ranching. Her mother had walked out on the family for unknown reasons just after Aaron died. And her father had just plain given up on life.

She sighed inwardly. Just as well she'd won Cash. No chance of a romantic entanglement there. He had the skills she needed—both in sheer muscle and in the knowledge of her store. She might never trust him to serve customers at the register as a clerk, but she had plenty for him to do even without handling money.

Cash hesitated as Alyssa unfolded a red-checked wool picnic blanket and dropped onto it with her legs folded underneath her. Only then did he seat himself, leaning on his forearm and stretching out one long, jeans-clad leg. She tried not to notice the way his bicep bulged under his T-shirt, but she found it difficult to avert her eyes.

She was a woman, after all. And once upon a time, she had been attracted to Cash.

Silently, she unpacked the picnic basket, passing him a plate, utensils and a cloth napkin before revealing the meal she'd made.

She'd cooked a turkey the day before and had prepared several sandwiches stacked high with all the fixings for them to feast on. She'd also wrapped the turkey legs as an extra treat. She'd made mashed potatoes and had topped them with a brown gravy. She'd prepared a cheesy broccoli casserole as a side and fudgy chocolate brownies for dessert.

She was starving. Her mouth watered just looking at the delicious spread. It had been a long time since breakfast and her stomach growled in anticipation.

Cash picked up a turkey leg. It was halfway to his mouth when Alyssa bowed her head to offer a short, silent prayer of thanksgiving to God, as she always did before a meal. When she opened her eyes, Cash had returned the turkey leg to his plate and was staring at her, his gaze, the vivid blue of the summer sky, wide with surprise.

Guilt speared her gut. She hadn't even asked if he wanted to pray with her, assuming, based on the rumors she'd heard, that he wouldn't be interested in offering thanks to God.

Heat flooded her cheeks. Where was her Christian charity? She should have at least asked if he wanted to share in the blessing.

But it was too late now. She gestured for him to eat and he picked up the turkey leg he'd previously dropped to his plate. He took a healthy bite, then another.

"Really good," he said between mouthfuls.

"Er—thank you," she replied, not quite sure what to do with his compliment. The warmth in his gaze made her feel as if fire ants were swarming over her skin. This situation was beyond uncomfortable.

And they hadn't even begun talking about the results of the auction yet. How was she supposed to explain what she expected from him?

They were eating in silence, which only made the situation worse. Could this be any more awkward? At least if they were talking she could try to lead the conversation toward her expectations.

A movement to her right caught her eye and she turned to see the stranger in the gray suit approaching, followed by a laid-back-looking fellow in a white T-shirt and ratty blue jeans. He carried a high-end camera with a long lens and a boxy camera case slung around his shoulder.

Without waiting for an invitation, the well-dressed

man crouched next to the picnic blanket. He shifted his gaze from Cash to Alyssa.

"So. Here's the deal," the man said, not bothering to introduce himself. "We're looking at a six-month hiatus while we put together Cash's publicity campaign. Our goal is to have him back in the saddle and the public's good graces by the National Western Stock Show in Colorado in January. With that in mind, this charity auction thing is our first event."

The man paused for her to acknowledge what he was saying, but rather than nodding, she shook her head. Even when Aaron was in rodeo, she'd never been interested enough to follow his career, so she knew nothing about the stock show he'd mentioned.

"You don't know of it? Well, never mind. That's not the point. Here's what's going to happen. Cash does whatever you have in mind for him to do, along with some carefully orchestrated acts of charity I'll prepare. I'll also line up some public appearances, so his fans can meet him. Something that emphasizes his hometown roots."

The man put an odd emphasis on "acts of charity," as if the words didn't mean what they were commonly meant to describe.

"I'm sorry—and you are?" Alyssa didn't like the way this man was looking at her—or talking about Cash, as if he was a piece of merchandise and not a man.

"Martin. Martin Brandt. Cash's agent and publicist," Martin answered in a clipped tone.

"I'm Alyssa Emerson."

He waved aside her introduction and continued as if she hadn't spoken.

"Our goal is to photograph Cash in the best possible light, capturing him working hard and doing good—for the sake of his new sponsors, of course."

Cash scoffed loudly, and Martin narrowed his deep-set eyes on him.

"*What* new sponsors?" Cash growled.

"*Potential* new sponsors, then," Martin corrected. "You've burned a lot of bridges, but I still think with the right publicity campaign we can get you back on track. You were once at the top of your game. You do exactly what I tell you, and I see no reason for you not to recover from your fall from grace."

"I'm sorry—*photograph*?" It was a lot to take in all at once, but the first part of the stranger's statement was what grabbed Alyssa's attention.

The guy with the camera just shrugged and smiled sheepishly.

Alyssa had won Cash in the auction, paying her hard-earned money for his services—not the other way around. So why did she suddenly feel like they were expecting, no—*demanding*—all take and no give?

This whole thing felt very much like they were ganging up on her, these three men, and she didn't like it one bit. If they thought she'd be a pushover, they had better think again.

"Yes. Photographs. By a photographer," Martin repeated. "Pete Drexler here is from *Rodeo Times*, the top rodeo magazine in the world. He'll be tailing Cash over the next few weeks and taking pictures we can use for good publicity. Which he desperately needs," Martin added.

Cash scoffed.

"The benefit to you being three months of free

labor," Martin pressed. "More, if I think it's necessary. I'm sure you'll see it my way when you consider all the facts."

Oh, yes, indeed. She could see. The picture was becoming increasingly clear. She snorted under her breath, but there was nothing funny about this situation.

She *was* being used. They intended to play upon her kindness to bring Cash back into the good graces of the rodeo world.

Not to mention she was now in possession, so to speak, of a sullen cowboy who clearly didn't want to be here in the first place. This was obviously not Cash's idea. It didn't take a genius to see Martin was twisting his arm, forcing him to do something he would rather have rejected.

It didn't matter what Martin said. This was never going to work.

Between keeping the store running, taking care of her ailing father and committing to a renovation that she now realized might be perfect on paper but in execution was going to be more complicated than she'd imagined, she was already in way over her head.

The last thing she needed was to worry about a photographer getting in the way all the time. The guy would be blocking the merchandise. Customers who might come into the store to browse wouldn't want Pete standing in their way.

She was worried that the mess and chaos of renovating the store for Kickfire was already causing her customers to look elsewhere for their hardware, outdoors and clothing needs. With most of the work still ahead of her, she couldn't afford to lose even a single sale, which might very well happen. Even if the townsfolk dared to brave the maze of new displays and boxes of stock around the store, she was certain they wouldn't want to be caught on camera for all the world to see.

They lived in a small town for a reason.

And she didn't even want to get started on Cash using *charity* for his own purposes.

Alyssa pressed her lips together into a tight line and narrowed her eyes on Martin before sliding her gaze to Cash, whose stony expression revealed nothing.

"I see," she said in a dry monotone. "But I'm going to have to decline."

Chapter Two

There was a big difference between humility and downright humiliation. Cash had known he was going to have to eat a lot of dirt when he came back to Serendipity, but Alyssa's words felt more like she was burying him in it, ten feet down.

He still wished he could walk away, but beggars didn't get to be choosers.

Rodeo was his life, and bareback riding was the only skill in which he truly excelled. Up until Aaron's death, he lived for the adrenaline that came along with the feel of a horse's muscles as it tried to fling him from its back. He reveled in the sound of the roaring crowd and the glare of the spotlights.

And yeah, he still wanted to be there. He wasn't quite ready to put his buckles on the shelf and succumb to the quiet life of a wrangler, which was the only job he would be qualified to do once his rodeo career ended.

Maybe someday he'd settle down, but not just yet.

Alyssa had bid on him and won him at this auction, and he wouldn't quickly forget hers was the *only* bid he'd had. He was obligated to assist her on whatever project she had in mind for him.

Because that was the promise he'd made by stepping onto the platform in the first place.

His word was one of the few things he had left, and he intended to honor it. Whatever she expected of him, he would do, if not willingly, then at least not grudgingly.

This was more of an opportunity than he deserved. This situation wasn't easy for a man who led with his ego, more often than not. The least *she* could do was agree to give him a little boost up in the process.

He was about to say something to that effect when Martin jumped in.

"What did you just say?" Martin snapped. "You're going to decline?"

Cash's agent was used to getting his own way, which was what made him so good at his job. Martin didn't take no for an answer. But he got the job done, and that was the bottom line.

"Was I not clear?" Alyssa countered.

Cash was impressed by her backbone. Not too many people dared take on Martin.

"I'm sorry, but I don't think it's a good idea to have a photographer lurking around my store right now. It would be bad for business."

Her gaze switched to Cash in silent appeal.

"Cash, help me convince your agent that we're not a good fit. It'll be in both of our best interests for you to work with someone else on your publicity scheme. I inadvertently put you in this awkward position by bidding on you, so I'll help you find someone else who will be more eager to work with you."

He shook his head. "There is no one else. Maybe you didn't notice back there." He gestured toward the stage, where the auction continued. Men were hooting, and women were cheering over whichever poor clod was out on display now. "People weren't exactly champing at the bit to pick me up at the auction."

She brushed a hand back through her hair and blew at a strand she missed. It floated upward and then down again, right into her eyes.

"Does that really surprise you? Rumors about your behavior on the rodeo circuit have been milling around here for months. The town does love gossip, you know."

He shifted his eyes away from her. "I figured as much. And you're right. I didn't expect any better."

"Martin? Can you give me some time alone with Cash?" Alyssa asked in a soft yet firm voice. It was a question, but not really a question. Not the way Alyssa delivered it.

Martin didn't look as if he was in any big hurry to capitulate to Alyssa, but when Alyssa shifted her gaze to him and narrowed her eyes on him, he reluctantly got to his feet and shrugged.

"Cash, I'm trusting you to convince her that this is in her best interest."

Anger flared in Cash's chest, mostly directed at himself and the circumstances he'd landed himself in.

How, exactly, was he supposed to convince Alyssa of anything?

He'd managed to royally screw up his life, and as a public figure, it wasn't surprising that his hometown neighbors knew what a mess he'd made.

Neither was he astonished they'd judged him for it. He didn't have any excuses for all he'd done. He was guilty on nearly every count, with the one exception of his connection with Sharee, the mother of his unborn baby. That woman had spouted off dozens of lies about him and completely wrecked his character, for no other reason than to get her own face in front of the camera.

No one other than Sharee knew that he'd immediately contacted her as soon as he'd heard, had attempted to accept his responsibility to his baby. He had offered his support and expressed his desire to be a true father to his child, only to be shot down by a woman who had no interest in him other than how she could use him to reach for her own celebrity status.

He'd tried everything he could think of. What more was there for him to do?

It was just another one of his failings, and one of his deepest regrets.

Alyssa waited until Martin was gone before she spoke.

"I've never been one to believe in rumors," she stated firmly. "I know how quickly things can get bent out of shape. Things are rarely as they seem."

Cash cringed so hard his muscles ached, and a cold sweat broke out on his forehead.

What was she going to do when she realized the rumors were true? Most of them, anyway. But the very worst was one that had never been spoken of at all—something he'd kept hidden from everyone. A secret that he'd have to conceal in the dark of his soul for the rest of his life.

That he was guilty of causing Aaron's death.

Alyssa's voice pulled him back to the present.

"I'd rather hear the truth directly from you, if you don't mind. I want you to tell me why you're here, and why you think your rodeo career tanked in the first place."

A spark of hope struck in his heart. She wanted to hear his side of the story. But that wouldn't matter. He quickly doused the flame.

"Why? What difference is it going to make what I have to say? What will make you believe me? Are you going to keep me on if I give you the answers you want to hear?"

"No. Yes." She paused and shrugged, rubbing her forehead thoughtfully. "Maybe."

He extended his other leg and stretched. This was going to take a while.

"Let me ask you something first," he said.

"Okay," she answered. She sounded hesitant, but she met his gaze head-on.

"One thing doesn't make sense to me. Why did you bid on me when you knew going into it what you were going to get?"

"What's that supposed to mean?"

A broken cowboy.

"My baggage. Even without a photographer following me around, I'm loaded with problems. As you said, you've heard the rumors. You know what I am. You realize people are going to judge you, too, just for associating with me."

"I'm not worried about that," she said, although her face drained of color. "I know who *I* am, and that's all that matters."

"You haven't answered my question," he reminded her.

She sighed.

"I bid on you partially because you are—*were*—

Aaron's best friend," she admitted. "I kept thinking about how he would feel if he saw you floundering up there, and I felt I owed it to his memory to rescue you."

She might as well have slapped him across the face, because that's how her words felt. That she would *rescue* him in Aaron's memory, after he—

No. He wouldn't go there.

He couldn't.

He wasn't going to think about it, much less talk about it. Not if he didn't want to end up on a bar stool, ordering a bottle of whiskey, which was the inevitable conclusion if he let his mind wander back to that night.

Instead, he lightened the mood and attempted to tease her, though he wasn't fully successful in his effort.

"Wow, thanks," he muttered sardonically. "And here I thought you picked me because I'm good-looking."

She snorted. "Inflate your own ego much?"

He tipped one edge of his mouth up in a half smile. "Hey, I'm just calling it as I see it. Remember, every morning I have to look at my reflection in the mirror."

The truth was, he *hated* what he saw when he looked in the mirror these days—blotchy skin, sunken eyes. The polar opposite of the good-looking youth he'd once been. Everyone else who laid eyes on him saw the same thing.

She apparently noticed the shift in his mood, because her lips turned to a frown.

"This isn't just about Aaron," she hastened to explain. "Yes, that was part of the reason I bid on you, but besides that, you really are the best fit for what I need done."

"How is that?" He couldn't imagine she believed he was good for anything.

"I'm doing some fairly major renovations with the store. I have to have everything done before the Christmas season starts this year because I've signed an exclusive contract with Kickfire to sell their products. Another pair of willing hands would be much appreciated."

"I'd be happy to help," he said, and meant it. "But if you don't mind my asking, what happened to Eddie? And your father? Aren't they helping in the shop?"

Her gaze dropped and her cheeks pinkened. "Eddie decided wrangling is more fun than adding up accounts at the end of the day. And my father—" She choked on the word and shook her head. "It doesn't matter. All you need to know is that I'm running the store myself for the time being."

He blew out a low whistle. "That's a lot to carry around on your shoulders."

"Mmm," she answered, but he couldn't tell whether she was agreeing with him or not. "I didn't anticipate having you around for more than a week at most, but a longer stay might not be all bad."

"Gee, thanks," he muttered, but he narrowed his eyes in concern when Alyssa's shoulders slumped.

"If I'm honest, I have to admit I'm bone tired from working six days a week with rare breaks."

She ran a hand down her face. Cash followed the movement with his eyes and for the first time noticed the tiny lines of strain in her expression.

"Back when you were in high school, you were employed part-time here at the store," she continued. "I suspect it won't take you very long to remember how we do things. Not much has changed since you've been here last. You already know how to set modules, restock, receive freight and keep the storage room in order, so I won't even have to teach you, will I? Or do you need a refresher?"

"I haven't forgotten," he assured her. "Working at Emerson's with Aaron is one of my best memories from high school. Your dad was good to me when I probably didn't deserve it. I wouldn't mind saying hello."

Her face suddenly blanched a pasty white and it looked as if she was choking on her breath, just as it had a moment ago when she'd mentioned her father.

Instinctively, he reached for her arm.

"Are you okay? What? What did I say?"

"Dad is ill," she said gravely. "That's part of the reason I'm running the store virtually on my own."

A tremor ran through her and Cash brushed his hand across her shoulder, comforting her as best he could, despite feeling awkward and powerless to do more for her.

"What's wrong with him?" he asked, his voice dropping lower than usual.

"I don't know if you heard anything about what happened to my family after Aaron died. It really affected my parents' relationship. The long and short of it is my mom evidently couldn't handle the pressure. She left town—and Dad."

Her voice cracked. "She left all of us. And she never looked back."

He sucked in a surprised breath between his teeth.

He *hadn't* known. Hadn't heard a word about it.

Having her mom abandon her? That couldn't have been an easy thing for Lizzie—*Alyssa*, he reminded himself, to go through, especially just after Aaron's death. Her mother. It didn't matter that Alyssa was an adult now. He couldn't even imagine what that felt like.

His stomach roiled. So much could happen in a mere six months. No time at all, and yet it felt like an eternity had passed.

A wave of guilt washed over him. Like the ripple created when he tossed a rock into clear water, his actions had caused so much turmoil. Cash was only now beginning to realize how much that one act—the proverbial rock he'd thrown into the water—had affected not only his life, but others', too.

Aaron had died. He had inadvertently hurt Alyssa—and her father. And no doubt Eddie, as well. The circle just seemed to keep growing.

This—*all* of this—was his fault.

"Dad hasn't recovered from Mom abandoning him," she whispered raggedly, continuing the story.

She cleared her throat. Her chocolate-brown eyes were glassy, but no tears fell.

"Like all of us, he'd depended on Mom for practically everything. She didn't just run the household. She supported everyone with her internal strength."

Alyssa sighed wearily. "Dad can't get along without her. I didn't know it at the time, but he recently admitted to me that he barely ate anything the first few weeks after Mom was gone. He lost a lot of weight, and it was only then that Eddie and I started noticing the changes in him. He can't sleep without a sedative. His health has taken a major nosedive and he's only a shell of the man he used to be."

"I'm so sorry. To lose your mom that way…"

Twin clefts appeared between her eyes. "We didn't

lose her. She isn't gone. She *walked away*. And she didn't look back. I don't even know if she considered how her actions would affect the family. She selfishly thought only of herself. Aaron's death might have been the last straw for her, but I suspect the situation went much further back than that."

"I'm so sorry," he repeated, not knowing what else he could say. No words could possibly act as a salve on Alyssa's heart. Cash of all people knew that.

Alyssa was in an even worse predicament than Cash had originally imagined. It was more important than ever that she agreed to accept his help. If Aaron hadn't died, her mother might not have left. Eddie might still be working in the store alongside Alyssa and their father. Cash had to try to make right the misery he'd caused, not that he would ever be able to do that.

"I'm surprised Eddie didn't stick around to help you," he said.

She scoffed. "I wish. Eddie spent last summer wrangling at a local ranch and decided *that* was what he wanted to do with his life, rather than running our family business as Dad had always intended. I'm happy for him, but—"

"But that leaves you high and dry."

She nodded. "Exactly."

"Which means you really do need my help."

She looked uncertain. He slid his hand down her arm and reached for her hand. Her gaze dropped to where their fingers met but she didn't remove her hand.

"You could have bid on anyone, but you bid on me. Let me help you."

"I want to," she said hesitantly. "But what about the photographer? The publicity? You must realize I don't have room in my life for extra hassles right now, however small."

A lightbulb went off in Cash's mind.

"Maybe that's precisely what you need."

She lifted her gaze to his and raised a brow. "Excuse me?"

"Publicity. Free promotion for your store. Pete's photos can do as much good for Emerson's as they can for my career. Surely that would be a boon to you, getting your face in front of the masses, so to speak. Let them know about the changes you're making."

Her face went from white to flaming red in a single breath of air.

"Not in this lifetime."

"What? Free publicity?"

"No. My face in front of people. That's not something I want to do."

"I think it's a great idea," he pressed, as the notion formed into solid concept. "You know all of those car salesmen and ambulance-chasing lawyers on television? They get their clients by using themselves to sell their products and services."

"I'm pretty sure everyone in Serendipity already knows I run Emerson's Hardware."

"Maybe so, but isn't part of the reason you're doing the renovation to bring in customers from surrounding towns? To be the go-to store for Kickfire Western wear products?"

"True," she admitted.

"It's solid marketing. Giving your store a face is a great way to personalize it," he said, "and draw in customers. That's the reason sponsors use me in their commercials. To give their products a face."

"Yes, but—"

He could see he wasn't convincing her. She didn't appear shy or introverted, but it had been a long time since they'd interacted on a personal basis. Maybe he was pushing her out of her comfort zone.

Whereas Cash—well, he loved the limelight.

"No, wait. I've got a better idea. *I* can do it," he crowed as the lightbulb in his head beamed brighter than the sun.

For the first time since Aaron's death, he felt excited about an idea, allowing it to break through the black cloud of his meager existence. He embraced the feeling. He wanted to do something other than nurse a tumbler of whiskey to numb his pain.

"Look. I'm trying my best to repair my reputation. If I clean up my act and become a positive influence—and wear Kickfire products—I can be your spokesperson. It'll help you gain more leverage with the store, and it will help me find new sponsors, once they see what a difference I've made for you and Kickfire."

"Maybe," she hedged.

He squeezed her hand. "It's the perfect plan. I help you, you help me."

He had every intention of helping her with far more than just offering his face for the camera and his public persona for the store. He aimed to receive inventory, move displays around, stock shelves and sweep the floors.

But she didn't have to know he'd be looking for extra ways to make her life easier.

This was the perfect way to redeem himself. He had developed his own set of moral principles to help him stay on the straight and narrow and he intended to follow those values to the letter.

Not that he ever could.

Not with the burden he carried.

He made a silent promise to himself. By the time he left Serendipity and went back to the rodeo, Alyssa would trust him.

If he couldn't win her over, there was no hope that the rest of the world would embrace him. Until he proved himself with her, he wasn't ready to go back to his old life.

"I can see what you're saying about my marketing plan," she acknowledged. "But before we go any further, there's one other issue, and I need you to tell me the truth."

His heart beat so hard he thought it might leap out of his chest.

"What do you want to know?" he finally asked, his voice raspy with emotions.

She stared at him for a long moment before speaking.

"How many of the rumors I've heard about you are true?"

Alyssa believed asking Cash about his recent past was reasonable, especially if she took him up on his offer to become the face of Emerson's Hardware. She couldn't have surprises lurking under every stone, revelations that could potentially harm the good name of Emerson's Hardware.

She hated to admit it, but what he'd said about her publicity strategy—or lack of one—made sense, even for as small a town as Serendipity. She intended to target several surrounding towns. As Cash had mentioned, people would come in from out of town once they heard she was selling Kickfire products. She'd recently created a website for the store so folks in the tri-county region and beyond could peruse weekly specials and feel compelled to visit her store. She was even looking into the prospect of shipping products directly to consumers.

That would majorly change the focus of her little shop and held the possibility of creating a substantial second stream of income. Her biggest concern was that once Cash fulfilled his obligation, she would once again be working the store alone. No matter how desperately Emerson's needed a boost in income, she didn't want to bite off more than she'd be able to chew.

At this point she wasn't planning to ship beyond the local area, but who knew what the future held?

One thing was certain—having a handsome cowboy hawking the goods—one who'd successfully sponsored other products in the past—would be a definite plus, especially for the Western wear.

But only if she could trust him.

And that was a big *if* right now.

If Cash was willing to lay it all out on the line and tell her the truth, and *if* he truly intended to strive to make up for his wrongdoings, she might be able to overlook the predicaments that got him into trouble in the first place.

Even if she had to put up with Martin's annoying interference and his own ideas for what a publicity campaign should entail, not to mention Pete's camera flashing.

Everyone deserved a second chance, didn't they?

Even a man like Cash, who'd fallen from grace in the rodeo world and was now struggling just to survive.

Maybe *especially* a man like Cash.

But only if he came clean now—literally and figuratively.

She waited, her breath catching in her lungs as Cash gathered his thoughts. He dropped his gaze and stared at the picnic blanket.

Was he going to explain what had really happened to him, or was he preparing to put on that false cowboy charm of his and try to find a way to gloss it over?

She suspected he was wearing a mask, and it was up to him to remove it and let Alyssa see what he looked like underneath the facade.

"Yeah. Okay." He paused and pursed his lips. "You deserve the truth if we're going to work together."

She nodded, encouraging him to continue.

"I don't know what you've heard. Why don't you tell me, and then I'll tell you how it really went down?"

"The drinking," she prompted, saying the first thing that came to mind. She might as well give it to him straight and hope he did the same with her.

"Yes." He didn't say another word, just caught her gaze and held it firm.

That was it?

Yes?

There had to be more to it than that.

"You did drink? You still do? I suppose what you do on your own time is your business, but I can't have you under the influence of alcohol while you're working at my store, especially with the renovations going on. It could be dangerous."

"I understand. And to answer your question, at one point I drank a lot, but now I don't."

"At all?"

"At all. Look. When I first entered the rodeo scene, I partied as much as the next cowboy, but once I lost Aaron, I lost my moral compass completely. I floundered, not only in my private life, but out in the arena. Alcohol was a way to dull my senses."

"I'm going to be forthright with you. After everything I heard about you, I half expected you to show up drunk today at the auction."

He frowned. "I won't ever do that to you. I promise I'm dry and will do everything in my power to remain that way. But I think it's only fair to tell you it's only been three days since my last drink. At this point I'm still going through physical withdrawal, not to mention emotional issues. It's not easy, but I'm detemined."

She pinched her lips. "I see."

She *didn't* understand the struggles he was facing. Not really. She'd never even tasted alcohol, much less been tipsy, nor had she ever spent any time around an alcoholic before, so she had nothing to gauge what Cash was pledging to her.

Could he really stop drinking cold turkey, and all on his own, as Martin had insisted?

"Is that a deal breaker?" He tilted his head and met her gaze. Like her, he didn't couch his question in sweet terms.

She considered his words for a moment, chewing the corner of her lip. After a long pause, she shook her head.

"No. Not necessarily. But know this. If you show up drunk on the job one time, I will kick you out the door faster than any bareback bronc ever did. You have exactly one opportunity to prove yourself. Do we understand each other?"

She knew she was being tough on him, and her demands wouldn't be easy for him to follow, but she wasn't about to start pulling punches now. She had her store to think of, before anything else, even her own emotions.

She understood herself well enough to know that if she worked with him, she would become entangled in his battle. She didn't have the strength, nor the good sense, to hold him at arm's length, especially if she saw him struggling. So the rules were as much for her as they were for him.

"Understood." His voice sounded like gravel, as if his throat was lined with sandpaper. "What else?"

She paused, opening and closing her mouth twice, about to speak and then stopping herself.

He tensed, and his gaze narrowed.

"Spit it out. Let's get everything out in the open now. Like you said. No surprises."

There was one other thing, but it was a touchy issue, perhaps even more so than his drinking. And Alyssa suspected Cash already knew what she was about to say.

"I heard there was a woman."

He exhaled and dropped his gaze to his hands, no longer willing or able to meet her eyes.

"Yes. I figured you would have heard about Sharee. She was all over the news with her smear campaign."

"Is that what it was?"

Alyssa thought she wanted the truth from him. But did she really want to hear it?

What if what Sharee had said was true? What if he *had* "knocked her up"—Sharee's words, not hers, and a phrase Alyssa found especially repugnant—and then refused to acknowledge his baby?

"A smear campaign?" He shrugged. "Yes and no."

"Cash?" she said, when he didn't continue.

"Yes, she is pregnant with my child. I willingly admit that I'm the father, and I take full responsibility for my actions, both then and now. But not one word of anything else she has blurted to the press is true.

"She's cast me in a very bad light, making it appear that I abandoned her when she told me I was going to be a father. The truth is, she didn't even bother to inform me she was pregnant. I had to hear *that* from the evening news."

He picked off his hat and tunneled his fingers through his thick black hair.

"Yeah, I've made a lot of mistakes, Alyssa. But I didn't walk out on her, because we never had a relationship. She was a buckle bunny and I was a rodeo cowboy too big for his britches. Which I guess makes me a jerk, so maybe she has that right. She pursued me, not the other way around. Not that I'm making excuses.

"We connected one time, and I was so drunk I barely remember."

She was trying not to judge Cash. But what kind of man got a girl pregnant like that?

Alyssa felt for the woman, buckle bunny or not. That Cash had a one-night stand with her only made the situation worse.

"And?" she pressed. "What now?"

"Are you asking me about my intentions?"

"I am."

He could tell her it was none of her business and he would probably be right. But if he did, she would send him on his way, auction or no auction.

"Believe me, I've tried to do right by her," he said, his voice cracking. "And my baby. As soon as I heard she was pregnant, I contacted her. There is no question in my mind that I'm going to pay child support, but it's more than that. I don't want my child to grow up without a father. I know I'm a mess right now and not the kind of man who would be a positive influence on a child. But I'd like to share custody after I get my life back together. Being a father is a huge motivation. Except Sharee has made it crystal clear she wants nothing to do with me, nor does she want me to have any part of our child's life."

His gaze dropped. "And who can blame her? Look at me. I'm hardly in any position to be a father, to take care of a baby. I'm a wreck.

"I have every intention of doing all I can for my baby—giving my financial support, at least, even if Sharee won't let me into my child's life in any other way." He groaned. "If I can't really be a father to him or her in the ways that really matter."

"But if it *is* your baby—"

"It is. I can't prove it right now, but I feel it in my gut, and the timing is right."

"Yes, but then don't you think…"

"Believe me, that's *all* I've been thinking about," he cut in. "I need to be a better man. Not just for the rodeo's sake, although there is that, since that's the only way I know how to provide for my baby. But the adjustments I intend to make in the way I live? In a few months my baby will be born. Talk about life changing. Suddenly it isn't all about me. My baby will be born soon."

His mouth curved up and a spark fired in his eyes at the mention of his baby's upcoming birth, but then he frowned and shook his head. "I only saw the ultrasound of the little bean because Sharee shared it on the news. She announced that she had just finished her first—trimester. Is that the right word? *Trimester*? I don't know much about pregnancy, and Sharee won't tell me anything."

Alyssa didn't much like the way this woman was treating Cash. Maybe he deserved it for how he'd treated her, but now there was a baby involved. They needed to put aside both their agendas for the child's sake.

It sounded like Cash wanted to do what was right, but if what Cash said about Sharee was true, she was using her baby for her own gain. It made Alyssa sick just to think about it.

"I'm sorry," she murmured.

"Don't be. It's all my own doing. I dug this hole, and now it's up to me to crawl out of it. I'm not anywhere close to being ready to be a father, but it's up to me now to *become* a good daddy. I know what I have to do now—and that starts with cutting out the whiskey."

"And that's why you've stopped drinking."

"I'm three days sober. That doesn't sound like much, but to me it feels like I'm climbing up the side of a steep mountain. I don't know if I'll ever reach the summit, but I have to try."

At least he was man enough to own up to his mistakes. But was that enough to keep him on the straight and narrow? Alyssa knew enough about alcoholism to know the path wasn't simple, and she sent up a short, silent prayer that God would be with Cash throughout the struggles he would face.

"So now you know the truth, it's up to you as to what you want to do with it. With me," he amended. "Are you willing to help me, not only with my rodeo publicity, but in regaining my life and integrity? Or do I need to look elsewhere?"

Alyssa thought of his agent, Martin, who stood just out of earshot, his gaze zoned in on them and a frown lining his face. At least the photographer who'd taken pictures of Cash at the auction and when they'd first shared the picnic was nowhere to be seen.

But Pete would be back, hanging around Cash, and no doubt getting in the way. Her customers would be bumping into him every time they turned around, and that was to say nothing of how chaotic the renovation might be.

She pressed her palms against her eyes where a headache was forming. It was a lot to consider, and she wished she had more time to think about it, but Cash needed an answer now.

And Cash wasn't the only one waiting for an answer. Even now, Martin was inching forward. Alyssa was certain he wouldn't walk away until he got what he wanted.

Her stomach churned, and she prayed she wasn't about to make the biggest mistake of her life.

"Okay, I'll help you," she said. "But I'll be watching you like a hawk. One mistake and you're gone. Is that clear?"

He gave a curt nod.

"Understood. And thank you." He tipped his hat at her.

"Don't thank me yet," she warned him. "This arrangement can end as quickly as it begins."

"I get it. It's all on me."

"I'll expect you to be at the store at 8:00 a.m. sharp Monday morning."

He stood, gesturing toward Martin. "I'd better tell him I'm sticking around so he can make arrangements for Pete to stay in town."

"Okay. And, Cash?"

"Yeah?" He turned, one dark eyebrow raised.

"Don't be late."

Chapter Three

Cash's head was slamming harder than the nails he was pounding with his hammer. Every movement was excruciating, like an ice pick repeatedly striking his temple. Cold sweat clung to his brow.

He'd been working for Alyssa for nearly a week, which meant he was close to ten days sober. He'd presumed he would be past any physical withdrawal symptoms. Mostly that was the case, but there were moments, like this one, where he felt like he had on his first alcohol-free day.

It was as if his body had a peculiar, regressive muscle memory. A cold sweat covered his skin, his entire body ached, his hands shook with tremors and his head throbbed incessantly.

He wished he had someone to ask about what he was experiencing, someone who had been through withdrawal and who would know if what he was feeling was normal. But he was too ashamed to participate in a twelve-step program or have a sponsor and, anyway, there wasn't a meeting within an hour's drive. He didn't have the time nor the inclination to make that much of a sacrifice.

No, he was going to conquer this all on his own. He'd used the internet to find out as much information on alcoholism as he could, facts he hoped would keep him from backsliding, but there were moments like this one that took every ounce of his willpower to battle.

He blew out an unsteady breath.

One sip and the shakes would go away. Two fingers in a tumbler and the black cloud that always covered his head would no longer threaten to rain on him.

But that was all an illusion, he reminded himself. Just because he numbed himself to the world didn't mean it wasn't there.

Alyssa had wasted no time putting Cash to work, and to his surprise, she'd put him on the payroll. He hadn't expected that, but he gratefully accepted it all the same. Every dime he pocketed was something he could give to his baby. He wouldn't say no to that.

And he was earning his keep. She needed six wooden storage shelving units built and four dozen new shelves cut, sanded and stained as part of her store renovation, using distressed wood to give the cabinets an old-fashioned appearance.

Building new shelves to mount boot displays on seemed a bit premature to Cash, since the new stock wasn't slated to arrive for another few months yet.

It hadn't taken much prompting for Alyssa to open up about her dreams for Emerson's. She really did love the store and the work she did. Once Cash had got her talking about the renovation, she'd become surprisingly animated, though the stress lines etched on her forehead deepened.

"I have the exclusive opportunity to represent one of the most well-known Western wear companies in the nation—the Kickfire brand. Not only their specialty line of clothing," she'd explained excitedly when she'd given him a tour of the store and described all the changes she wanted to make, "but their hats and boots, as well."

"That's awesome," he told her. "They're one of rodeo's biggest sponsors. They even have a bareback bronc by the name of Kickfire."

"It is a big honor for me to have pulled in the brand, but it's also going to be quite a challenge. I've promised the company that my renovation will be done before Christmas. Ideally, their product line will be stocked before Black Friday, so folks can buy Kickfire Western wear to use as Christmas presents."

"The people in Serendipity and surrounding towns are going to be stoked," he assured her.

"I hope so. But I still have so much to do. I want to patch the drywall and repaint all the walls before the shelves you're building can be hung. I'm also hoping to replace the wood flooring, if the budget allows. At this point some parts of the renovation are still very much up in the air."

As far as Cash was concerned, she still had plenty of time before the beginning of the Christmas season to complete her detailed vision, but Alyssa appeared as anxious as if the entire load of stock was heading her way now.

Apparently, she wasn't as certain as Cash was that she could pull it off. It *was* a lot to do. She wanted the grand reopening ready to go on Black Friday, with her store completely renovated, newly stocked and thoroughly decked out with Christmas decorations.

Bah humbug.

That was one part of her scheme Cash could do without. He didn't have much use for Christmas and everything that went along with the season, and it was going to be pure torture for Alyssa to remind him of her holiday goals ten times a day, every day.

He'd be gone long before the Christmas season started, of course, but she was already talking about Christmas as if it were tomorrow. He didn't even want to think of how obnoxiously her cup would runneth over with holiday cheer the closer she got to December 25.

Peace on Earth and goodwill toward men. Bright lights and Christmas carols. Deck the halls and joy to the world.

Stuff and nonsense, that's all it was.

What was there to be cheerful about? This world and everything in it only caused strife and sorrow.

He was proof of it.

Aaron was proof of it.

Well, it wasn't his problem. He had enough quandaries of his own to deal with, without accidentally allowing his relationship with Alyssa to become personal in any way. He was always ultra-aware of her whenever she was in the same room with him, but it was better for everyone that he kept his distance from Aaron's sister.

With his resolve firmly in place, he turned his full attention to the work at hand. When she'd first mentioned building display cases, he'd told Alyssa that he could hammer and saw, but a carpenter, he was not. The whole project was going to be slow going, but he supposed that was making it easier for Pete to capture pictures of him covered in sawdust with a pencil behind his ear.

Working hard on his charity project, for what that was worth.

After Cash posed for the camera with a hammer in his hand, Pete indicated he was taking a break and Cash was able to relax and actually enjoy working with his hands. He gauged the next board out with his tape measure and cut it to size with a circular saw, nodding to acknowledge Alyssa as she approached him.

She'd been busy with a steady stream of customers all morning. A couple of times he'd considered asking her if she'd like him to help out at the register. It had been a few years since he'd worked at Emerson's, but he thought he remembered how to use the till.

But since she didn't ask, he didn't offer. He hadn't shown himself to be the most stand-up guy in the past few months. She probably didn't trust him around money.

Not that he could blame her. *He* wouldn't trust him around money.

So instead, he did his best to keep himself and Pete out of the way of the flow of shopper traffic. Some of his old friends and neighbors stopped to say hi, which surprised him, especially after the public shunning he'd received at the auction.

Slade and Nick McKenna, ranchers who'd both competed in rodeo with him when they were in high school, stopped by to say hey. Cash had expected to feel uncomfortable, but his friends treated him as they always had, laughing and joshing around.

He supposed he was old news now, which was just as well.

He set aside the saw and picked up his hammer, ready to finish nailing the shelving unit together.

"How are you doing back here?" she asked, examining the wooden case he was currently building. "I'm impressed at how much you've been able to get done with Pete constantly in your face snapping your picture. Doesn't that bother you?"

He shrugged. "I'm used to it."

"The cabinet looks nice and sturdy."

"Ha, ha. It ought to be." He lifted his hammer to strike the next nail. "I've been using more nails than is probably strictly necessary. Remember, I'm a cowboy, not a carpenter."

"It looks good all the same."

Her words of praise surprised and pleased him, and his fingers slipped, bringing the ball of the hammer straight down on his thumb.

"Ow," he grumbled before he could stop himself. He held up the offended appendage and shook it out.

Alyssa reached for him. She pulled his hand down and examined his thumb. "I'm so sorry. This is all my fault. I distracted you, didn't I?"

That ship had already sailed a long time ago. Alyssa was distracting by her mere presence, which was probably why he'd already smacked his thumb more than once today. He might be trying to build an emotional barrier between them, but he wasn't immune to her pretty face, especially when she smiled.

"Don't worry about it." He tried to shrug it off. "It's not the first time today I've slipped up," he admitted, gritting his teeth to grin at her and realizing it probably looked more like a grimace. He didn't want to be a baby about it, no matter how much his thumb was throbbing. He was too much of a man to ever admit how much pain he was really in.

"Oh, no. Cash. You should have said something."

"Nothing to say," he muttered. "It's all good."

It would take more than a few splinters and slamming the hammer into his thumb to keep him from his task. He would take a couple of aspirin when he got home.

His head was throbbing louder than his thumb, anyway. He had so much on his mind that it was no wonder his brain felt as if it were about to explode.

Mollifying Martin and bringing his rodeo skills up to par, for one thing. Another, infinitely more significant reason for his stress was that he couldn't get a hold of Sharee. She wasn't answering his calls and now her voice mail box was full.

What were her plans for their baby? He suspected she was avoiding him, so she wouldn't have to answer that question.

He blew out a frustrated breath. Hitting his thumb was little more than pain transference, if he wanted to look at it that way. And Alyssa was a nice diversion.

He picked off his hat and wiped his forehead with the sleeve of his shirt.

Her lips twitched.

"What?"

"Forgive me." Despite her best efforts, a giggle escaped her lips. "I know you're in pain. It's terrible of me to laugh, but…but you…you…"

She waved her hand toward his forehead, the cutest little snort escaping her lips.

He arched his brows.

She covered her face as another giggle escaped her.

He reached up and brushed his forehead with his fingers. He pulled his hand away to see grime caking the tips. He suspected what had started as a swirl of sweat and sawdust now had three distinct finger marks treading through it, like an animal's track.

What now?

He couldn't think of a way to fix the problem without making it worse. He obviously couldn't use his gunked-up shirtsleeves, and he didn't carry a handkerchief.

"Hold on a second," she said, jaunting off to the bathroom just inside the stockroom. She returned a moment later with a couple of wet paper towels and two dry ones, as well.

"Here. Let me." She leaned on tiptoe to wipe his forehead clean and then handed him the dry paper towels to finish mopping up.

"Dirty work, I guess," she teased.

"No worse than rodeo. Anyway, I'm enjoying doing something different for a change. Working with my hands is fulfilling. It's a new experience for me to build something from nothing but raw materials. And I think I'm getting the hang of it. Give me a day or two and I'll be a regular Mr. Fix It."

"I hope so. I don't need an employee out on an injury so quickly after hiring you."

"It would take more than me slamming a hammer into my thumb to put me on the injured list. And you bid on me at an auction, which isn't exactly the same thing as hiring me for a job, as grateful as I am that you're paying me."

She made a vague gesture. "Six of one..."

She paused. "Actually, I came over to ask you if you wanted to break for lunch and grab some takeout from Cup O' Jo's Café."

"I'll never say no to a good meal." He smiled down at her. "Let me tidy up this mess a bit while you call Jo with our order, and then I'll go pick it up. Chance's daily special? Don't forget dessert."

Chance Hawkins was Jo Spencer's nephew and head cook at the café, while his wife, Phoebe, was well-known for her homemade pastries.

"Sounds like a plan."

Alyssa moved back behind the front counter and picked up the phone to call Cup O' Jo's Café. Cash filled his arms with random fragments of leftover boards and let himself out the back door into the alley where the Dumpster was located, shared by several stores on the east side of Main Street.

He flipped the lid back and was just about to toss his armful of wood shards into the bin when he heard a tiny, distraught mewl.

He froze, suddenly alert.

It was a cat—or at least he thought it was, and it sounded as if it was in distress.

But where was it?

He had far too much to do today to spend time looking for a random cat that either belonged to someone else or likely was feral, out roaming around back here. It wasn't his business or his pet, but he couldn't push away the niggling feeling there was something wrong.

He'd always followed his gut. It seldom led him wrong—even if it was just about a cat.

Dumping his armful of wood on the ground next to

the trash container, he turned around slowly, his gaze sweeping across the back of the building. It was clean, save for a few empty crates, and there weren't many places for a cat to hide.

He swiveled back the way he'd come and walked around the Dumpster, crouching to look underneath.

"Here, kitty, kitty," he murmured in the high voice men reserved for animals and babies. "Where are you?"

His ears picked up two more soft mews, one right on top of the other.

Was there more than one cat?

Inside the Dumpster, *maybe*?

Cautiously, he peeked over the edge and into the bin, trying not to make any noise that would startle a cat.

Sure enough, a mama cat was curled on her side on top of a broken-down box, nursing five tiny newborn kittens. The inadvertent distress calls had come from the little ones.

If he hadn't heard the kittens' mewling when he had, he might have—

His gut lurched painfully. The thought made him sicker to his stomach than he already was.

He'd been just about to pitch an armful of heavy and some sharply pointed lumber right on top of the poor mama cat and her newborn kittens.

"Thank God," he murmured before even realizing he was praying. It had been a while since those words had left his mouth, but he didn't want to take them back.

Lifting his hat and scratching the back of his neck, he went back into the shop and waited until Alyssa hung up the phone with Jo.

"Hey, Alyssa," he called from the stockroom. "We've got a—*situation* here."

"What's up?" she asked, approaching him. When she saw his face, her gaze filled with concern.

"There is—I almost—" he stammered, wiping his clammy hands down the front of his shirt. "It's not the major catastrophe it could have been. And now—I'm thinking you might like what you see. Maybe it would be easier if I just show you."

He gestured for her to go ahead of him out the back door and into the alley.

"I was about to toss an armful of wood scraps into the trash bin when I heard mewling."

"A cat?" She looked puzzled. "What's the big deal about a cat? We have several feral cats roaming around here."

"True." He shrugged and grinned mischievously. "But I found this one *inside* the Dumpster."

"It's a good thing you heard him before you tossed a pile of wood on him. He could have gotten hurt. Did you shoo him away?"

"Um…no, I didn't. And it's a her," he said, his grin widening. "Take a look for yourself."

Alyssa peered over the top of the bin and she broke into a smile that lit up her whole face. She was beaming like sunshine on a cloudless Texas summer day.

"Kittens," she exclaimed. "Newborn, by the looks of it. Their little eyes aren't even open yet."

"Brand-new to the world," he affirmed, trying not to be affected by the way Alyssa's voice had softened when she spoke of the kittens.

"Thank the good Lord you heard them in time." She

looked toward the sky when she spoke, and Cash knew her words were really a prayer.

As for Cash, he'd abandoned his faith in the Lord the day he'd left Serendipity in the dust, which was why his own instinctive prayer for the kittens had come as such a surprise to him. As a young man who'd thought he was invincible, he'd had no use for God. Now, after all he'd done, he couldn't understand why God would have any use for him. But he was thankful he'd found the litter before he'd accidentally hurt them.

"I know I'm stating the obvious here, but we've got to move them," she determined. "They are in danger here. I know the mama cat probably doesn't want us to bother her. We don't even know if she's from around here. It's possible she's feral, which will make things more complicated. But we can't very well leave them in the Dumpster. There's no telling when someone else will toss a bag of trash into the bin without hearing them the way you did."

"I agree," he said, nodding. "But what are we going to do with a mama cat and a litter of kittens?"

"Why, adopt them, of course." Alyssa's grin widened, then faltered. "At least for the time being. Maybe one of them can become our new store mascot."

Cash chuckled. "The feline face of Emerson's Hardware."

Not for the first time in her life, Alyssa's mouth had worked faster than her head. That seemed to be happening to her more and more often recently.

She'd never had a pet before, much less a cat, and she had no clue how to care for a litter of kittens. But it wasn't as if she had a choice. She couldn't just leave them in the bin where they might get hurt, and the only idea that came to her was to take them inside her store—for the time being, anyway. She didn't necessarily have to keep them, but in truth, she'd fallen in love with the sweet kitties the moment she saw the tiny bundles of fur.

"You want to keep them here at the store?" Cash asked dubiously, drawing a hand down his darkly stubbled jaw.

"I think that's reasonable, at least for now. We'll need to ask around to see if anyone is missing a cat, of course."

She shrugged. "I suppose I could take them back to my apartment, if you think that would be a better scenario. The only thing is, I work here nine-plus hours a day, six days a week, so I will be able to keep a better eye on them here at the store. The shop does get noisy sometimes, but I think they'll do okay in the storeroom. When they're older we can keep them behind the counter."

"Kittens will be a big draw for the customers," he said. "Giving them an extra reason to stop by and visit Emerson's. I suspect it will be easy to adopt the kittens out when the time comes."

They hadn't even technically rescued the kittens, and yet already the thought of adopting them out made Alyssa's heart drop. Not that she could keep an entire litter of kittens. That was out of the question.

Maybe one, though. If they weren't claimed by the mama cat's owner.

"The mother is so pretty. Such unique coloring. She doesn't look like a stray, but you never know. We should take a picture of her and put it on a poster in the window. Someone is bound to be missing their pet."

"Good point. But at the moment, our biggest issue is figuring out how to rescue the litter."

"I don't know the first thing about caring for cats, never mind kittens. I'll look it up on the internet once we've got them inside. For now, let me see if I can rustle up a couple of blankets. I think I have an empty box around here somewhere that might work as a bed for them."

She ducked inside and took a couple of soft, new snuggle-blankets off the shelf, removing the tags and placing them near the cash register so she could ring the blankets up later. She found a short-sided box and situated it in the warmest corner of the storage room, and arranged the blankets for the litter's comfort.

Cash entered the stockroom with two kittens tucked into his shirt. Alyssa's heart leaped at the sight of the handsome cowboy carrying the newborn kittens with such gentleness. Kindness and compassion lined his expression, softening his features.

There was something innately attractive about a man rescuing a helpless baby animal—or in this case, five plus the mama, and when his stress lines receded, it was easy for Alyssa to remember how handsome he was way back when. How good-looking he would be now, were he not worse for the wear and tear of life.

"Here are the first two," he said, gently placing them in the basket. "They're so helpless. Their eyes aren't even open yet and they mewled like crazy when I picked them up. They didn't want to be taken away from their mama, that's for sure. I hope I didn't frighten them too much."

Cash crouched beside the box and ran the tips of his fingers across the kittens' soft fur before rising back to his feet. "I'd better hurry and get the other three kittens. I'm saving the mama cat for last because I suspect she's going to be the most difficult to deal with."

He laughed. "I don't think Mama Kitty understands that we want to help her."

He flashed the back of his left hand. Angry red claw marks etched the skin.

"Your poor hand," Alyssa murmured sympathetically. "Between the cat and your hammer…" She was serious, but she added a teasing note in her voice.

He gave her a playful growl. "Rub it in, why don't you?"

She chuckled. "Can I help it if you are a walking, talking accident just waiting to happen?"

Who also happens to save kittens.

He snorted. "That about sums it up."

Their gazes met and locked for a moment before she looked away, pretending to busy herself with the kittens in the box. Her heart was rapidly beating, and she took a deep breath, concentrating on slowing her pulse to its normal rate. She tried to tell herself that it was just the adrenaline of having found the litter of kittens, but deep inside, she knew better.

Cash left to retrieve the other three kittens before bringing in the mother cat. Given the war wounds he already bore from tussling with the mama cat, Alyssa half expected him to bring her in holding her at arm's length and away from her sharp claws. Instead, he'd cradled her against his chest and was stroking her head.

"She doesn't look so dangerous now," Alyssa said.

"It appears you've made a new friend. Look—she's purring."

"She'll be even happier once I get her situated with her babies."

He stooped to place the cat into the box with the kittens and remained there for a moment, watching the blind, cuddly balls of fluff instinctively crawling over each other to reach their mama.

"Mama Cat is such a pretty color," Alyssa remarked. "I wonder what it's called?"

Cash shrugged. "Fancy, whatever it is."

"That's it," Alyssa exclaimed, clapping her hands with glee.

"What is?" Cash jerked to his feet at her sudden delighted outburst, a puzzled expression on his face.

"Fancy. I was just thinking about how we needed to call her something, give her a name—until her owner claims her, that is. We can't keep calling her Mama Cat. That's just weird."

He raised one dark eyebrow.

"Fancy is the perfect name for her." She leaned down to run her palm across the cat's long, multicolored fur. "What do you think of that, Fancy?"

The cat meowed twice in response.

Cash laughed. "I guess that's a yes, then."

Alyssa pulled out her cell phone to see if she could identify the cat's breed and hair color.

"I've found out what the unique coloring is called," she said after she'd typed in a few key words. "Fancy is a calico. The color appears in many breeds of cats, though, so I'm not sure about that yet."

"Interesting that only one of her babies has the same coloring as Fancy," Cash remarked. "You'd think they'd all be the same, right? Or maybe one or two colors and patterns like their parents. But the rest of these kittens look nothing like Fancy, or each other, for that matter."

"I wonder why that is?" Alyssa mentally added that question to her ever-growing list of things she suddenly wanted to learn about cats. Of course, the care and feeding of a mama cat and a litter of kittens was at the top of that list. The rest could wait until later.

"It must be some kind of a genetic mystery," Cash said. "You know, like how human parents who both have brown eyes can have a blue-eyed baby."

"I'll do more online research later, but right now we need to concentrate on the basics," she said. "Water and cat food for Fancy, and a litter box."

"Good thing you own Emerson's," Cash said with an amused gleam in his blue eyes, gesturing to the feed department, which contained everything from horse barley to kitten food, as well as an assortment of pet supplies. "You don't even have to visit a different store to get supplies for your new kittens."

Alyssa noticed that Cash had lost his broody attitude once he'd come across the litter of kittens. He'd been pleasant over the week he'd worked for her, but she could tell his surly attitude had been brimming just beneath the surface, something Alyssa suspected he always carried with him, maybe without even realizing it.

Now his gruff manner was replaced by gentle empathy for the kittens.

Best of all was the way one corner of his lips tugged up in a half smile as he watched the tiny furballs sleeping all curled up against their mama. That grin changed his whole countenance, the difference between midnight and dawn. He was quite attractive when he smiled.

She didn't want to notice.

She didn't want her stomach to flutter in his presence. Not like it had when she was a silly love-struck teenager. This was different, and hazard signs were all over this road.

BEWARE, they warned, their blinking lights flashing. SHARP TURN AHEAD.

Chapter Four

It had been an interesting two weeks, he thought as he let himself into the store on Sunday morning.

"Do you still remember how to use this old dinosaur of a cash register?" Alyssa had asked him yesterday.

"Not much to remember, as I recall, other than counting change, and I think I can handle that," he'd replied, trying not to let her see how stunned he was that they were having this conversation.

And then she'd really knocked him for a loop.

"I've got something for you," she'd said, holding one hand behind her back. She'd had a twinkle in her eye and a smile on her face.

"What is it?" he'd asked, jabbing from side to side to try to grab her hand as she sashayed away from him with a laugh.

Suddenly her expression had become serious. "I'm going to give this to you because you have done everything I've asked from you and more. Since you volunteered to look in on the kittens on Sundays, you'll need to have this."

She withdrew her hand from her back. A sparkling new door key hung from her fingers.

She couldn't possibly have known what that meant to him. His first two baby steps toward trust. He got all choked up even now, thinking about it.

He liked that he could give Alyssa the opportunity to enjoy her Sunday at church and with her family. He enjoyed the work at the store, and with careful budgeting for food and lodging, he intended to stash away most of his earnings for his baby.

Sooner or later, Sharee was going to have to respond to him, or else he was going to show up at her door unannounced. He was the baby's father, and he suspected Sharee was trying to rob him of both the responsibility and the pleasure of taking care of his child.

That wasn't going to happen.

He was even starting to picture what his life would be like if he settled down in Serendipity—at least in the off-season. If he continued to get his life together and didn't mess up, perhaps he could retain shared custody of his baby.

The thought both elated and frightened him, but he knew that his friends and neighbors in Serendipity would offer support he wouldn't find elsewhere.

Why hadn't he seen the benefits of living in a small town until now? He'd matured, he supposed. And it had turned out that living off adrenaline wasn't all it was cracked up to be.

He had seriously considered not returning to rodeo at all, and remaining in Serendipity, though he hadn't asked Alyssa about the possibility of continuing to work for her.

She was such a sensitive individual that she might

agree for altruistic reasons, and the last thing he wanted to do was pressure her into anything.

No. He needed to stick to the original plan. The whole reason he was in Serendipity in the first place was to polish his tarnished image, so he could return to rodeo. Bareback riding was ultimately his strongest skill set. He would need to provide for his baby, and rodeo was the best way he knew to do that.

He wouldn't return to the rodeo circuit until January, giving him ample time and opportunity to brush up on his bareback-riding skills. When he did make his comeback, he would make sure he was wildly successful. He boarded a couple of horses in Serendipity's public barn and corral and practiced his skills in the evenings and on his days off.

Serendipity had become his safe place, and Alyssa a close friend. She was the one person he could really talk to—although of course she still didn't know about the darkest burden he carried in his soul. He wasn't ready to tell her and doubted he would ever be. He protected and guarded his relationship with Alyssa because he feared if she knew the truth she'd send him packing so fast his head would spin.

He couldn't take that risk, no matter how tempting it was to unburden himself.

Today, at least, he wouldn't even have to worry about fighting the urge to blurt out his secret, because he wouldn't see Alyssa at all.

He yawned widely as he walked into the back room to check on Fancy and the kittens. He'd been an only child, and his parents had moved to Scottsdale, Arizona, for their retirement, so he was living alone when he wasn't working, renting a cabin at the Howell's Bed-and-Breakfast, and the silence sometimes got to him.

Alyssa had invited him to visit the community church with her on more than one occasion, and he was seriously considering going back. Living in Serendipity with its slow pace had allowed him to ponder his life and where he would be going from here. Time had solidified his moral code and kept him walking the straight and narrow.

For the first time in years, maybe since childhood, the idea of being in a relationship with God wasn't quite as far-fetched as it once had seemed. It appeared to be the natural next step in his quest for a better life, but he still wasn't quite ready to darken the door of a church. Not until he was certain he could live up to the standards he'd created for himself.

As Alyssa had suggested that first day on the community green, the gossip hive had moved on to the Next Big Thing less than a week after the auction and he was old news.

The problem was that he was still judging himself. He alone knew how many times he'd been ready to sneak off and find a liquor store. He still balked at the idea of attending an Alcoholics Anonymous meeting, but he did see the wisdom in having a sponsor to talk to, someone who understood his addiction.

The corner of his mouth turned up in a half smile as he watched the kittens crawling over each other to be close to Fancy. Spending time with kittens wasn't exactly the same as human contact, but at least they were furry and cute, and he could cuddle them in his arms. Their eyes were open now, tiny sharp teeth were emerging, and they were starting to toddle around on their own.

He might not be in church right now with the rest of the townsfolk, but he experienced a sense of peace nonetheless. He liked the quiet. Or the relative quiet, since the kittens were mewling.

Emerson's, along with the rest of the businesses on Main Street, was closed on Sundays, which might have appeared strange to an outsider. But Cash had grown up in Serendipity and couldn't imagine it any other way.

He'd laughed when Pete, in the middle of a photo shoot with Cash and the kittens, had mentioned how odd and backward it was, like a throwback to the nineteenth century. The town, with its clapboard sidewalks and old-fashioned storefronts, really did look like something from another era.

Cash filled Fancy's dish with a can of cat food and mashed up a second one for the kittens to share. They were starting to wean themselves from their mother and were anxious to feast on the food Cash offered.

Cash pressed his back against the wall and slid down until he was seated next to the box containing Fancy and the kittens, immediately scooping the little black kitten with white-tipped paws into his lap.

"Hello, Maus," he said, scratching behind the kitten's ears.

No one had come forward to claim the litter, but he knew—and *Alyssa* knew—they would have to be adopted out to others when the time was right.

It was inevitable. Alyssa couldn't keep a handful of full-grown cats inside her shop. And yet despite her smiles, he'd occasionally catch a glimpse of sadness in her eyes when she looked at them.

By the second day at the store, the kittens had all been named. The white one was Smudge, the calico was Aspen, the tortoiseshell was Bishop and the gray kitten was Socks.

Cash was surprised how invested he'd become in the fluff-ball litter. He liked all the kittens, but he'd personally christened his favorite Maus. The tiny kitten's eyes were a mesmerizing blue-gray color that made Cash beam and Alyssa exclaim in delight.

All the kittens were adorable, and Cash had no doubt that even though they lived in the country where barn cats were a dime a dozen, they would have no problem finding homes for these little bundles of fur.

His thoughts turned to the day after they'd first found the litter. They'd put out a notice on the door of the shop and asked around town to find out if anyone was missing their cat, but no one had claimed Fancy, so as Alyssa had first suggested, Fancy had become the unofficial store mascot. Shoppers often stopped by with their children to exclaim over the kittens and they became a big draw.

"We've totally gotta do this," Pete had insisted when he'd found out about the litter.

"What? Me and a cat?" Cash had asked dubiously. "What's the big deal about that?"

"You and a *kitten*," Alyssa had countered. "Trust me when I say a picture of you and Maus—Cash's favorite kitten—will go a long way in scrubbing up your image. Ladies love seeing men with kittens."

He didn't care overmuch what ladies in general thought, but he did wonder if this photo shoot had any effect on Alyssa. Even though she was occasionally busy with customers, she'd watched as much of the photo shoot as she could. He'd felt ridiculous posing with a kitten on his shoulder, on the ground pawing at his jeans or tucked into his T-shirt. Whenever he'd felt Alyssa's eyes on him, it had taken his mind off what he was supposed to be doing and he'd felt as if the temperature in the room had skyrocketed. Surely his face must have been flushed.

When his gaze had sought hers, he couldn't tell if she'd been smiling or smirking.

"Good job," she'd announced when he was finished. "Way to show your softer side."

Cash had snorted. Talk about ridiculous. What did cradling a cat in his arms have to do with establishing a man's personality?

Everyone liked kittens, didn't they?

Cash didn't *have* a soft side. His heart was as hard as stone.

The kitten currently curled on his forearm mewled his displeasure and bumped his head into Cash's palm, only stopping to purr when Cash stroked his fingers across Maus's fur.

Cash laughed. "Sorry, little guy. My mind wandered. You want my full attention, don't you?"

If he had his way, Cash would adopt Maus himself, but he had nothing to offer a cat, or any other living thing, for that matter.

Traveling the rodeo circuit was no place for a pet, even—or maybe especially—one as independent as a cat. Maus was already starting to display his individuality from his brothers and sisters, and Cash often chuckled at his feistiness. Maus reminded Cash of himself.

From what he and Alyssa had read in their research

about kittens, during the next eight weeks they would show great progress in their growth and personalities. He couldn't wait to watch sweet Maus mature, but he reminded himself not to get too attached to the little guy. When the kittens were weaned, one of Emerson's many customers, maybe a family with little children, would become Maus's new owner.

And Cash might never see the kitten again.

His chest filled with an unrecognizable emotion as he placed Maus back in the box with his brothers and sisters. Before, part of the allure of the rodeo circuit was being in a different town every week, often in a different state.

Nothing the same. Everything new and exciting.

But these last couple of weeks working at Emerson's with Alyssa, he'd experienced another side, a slower, gentler way of life, but no less rich for its leisurely pace.

His cell phone buzzed from the back pocket of his jeans. Not too many people had his number, and even less would be interested in calling him for any reason. It was probably Martin, demanding an update on Cash's progress with the publicity campaign.

He glanced at the screen and was surprised to see Alyssa's name. He'd given her his cell number when he'd first started at Emerson's, so she could get in touch with him if she needed him at the store or for other work-related communications.

"Alyssa?" he asked, curiosity piquing his interest. Why was she calling him on a Sunday?

"Cash."

All she said was his name, but he could clearly discern the note of panic in her voice.

"Alyssa. What is it? What's wrong?"

"It's Daddy," she said, her breath catching on a sob.

A pure shot of adrenaline jolted through Cash, a feeling his body naturally embraced even as anxiety constricted his chest.

"What happened?"

Cash had always liked Edward Emerson. Cash hadn't exactly been a model student and he had been known to get into trouble a time or two. But Edward had given Cash a job when many others turned him down as being too much of a risk. He'd planned to go over to the house and say hello, but the past two weeks had been busy.

"He fell."

"Is it serious?"

"I don't know. I wasn't here when it happened. I'm afraid to move him. He won't let me call an ambulance. I can't get him up on my own, and I'm not even sure I should. I came over to the house to make lunch for us and I found him lying on the floor in the kitchen, crying out in pain. Eddie is out on a roundup this weekend and out of cell phone range."

"Give me five," Cash said, already rushing out the door and locking it behind him. He didn't have any idea why she'd think to call him, but now wasn't the time to ask. "Hang in there, Alyssa. I'll be right over."

His heart hammered brutally, and his mind spun with life-threatening scenarios as he jogged down the street toward the housing complex where Alyssa's father lived. He half wished he'd brought his truck this morning, but he could probably make it faster on foot, anyway.

When he reached the Emersons' house, he let himself in without knocking.

"Alyssa?"

"In here," she called from the kitchen.

Cash dashed toward the sound of her voice. When he rounded the corner into the kitchen, he found Alyssa's father sprawled across the well-worn rose-patterned linoleum, Alyssa on her knees bending over him and supporting his head.

Cash was shocked by Edward's appearance, and it wasn't only because he'd obviously taken a bad fall. Cash regretted that he hadn't made it a point to stop by earlier.

The old man's face was drawn and pale, his thinning white hair poking up in tufts. Though it was the middle of summer, he was dressed in thick flannel pajamas. His feet were clad only in socks, and Cash suspected that might be part of the reason he had slipped on the slick linoleum.

Cash brushed a comforting hand across Alyssa's shoulder as he crouched down by Edward and she offered him a grateful nod.

"What happened?" he asked. He was addressing both of them, but his gaze fixed on Edward.

"He was leaning over to pick up a dishrag he'd dropped, and he lost his balance," Alyssa answered.

"Stupid," Edward muttered, his voice raspy and hoarse. He tried to sit up and then groaned in pain and rested his head back onto Alyssa's lap.

"No, Daddy. It's not your fault. It was an accident. It could have happened to anyone." She tenderly brushed her father's hair out of his eyes. Tears flooded her cheeks.

Cash's chest clenched. He wanted to make those

tears go away. Fix her problem. But that was easier said than done.

"You didn't call an ambulance?" Cash confirmed.

"No," Edward snapped. "No ambulance. No emergency room, either. I'm fine. Besides, it would take an hour to get to the nearest hospital, and all they'll do is tell me I have bumps and bruises. Like that ain't obvious."

Cash didn't know about the "fine" part, but Edward was right about the hospital. Unless it appeared that something was broken, he'd probably be better off, and a great deal more comfortable, just going straight to bed and resting.

"Can you sit up?" Cash asked.

"What if he has a concussion?" Alyssa whispered.

"I'm still here, and I can hear you perfectly," Edward said. He chuckled coarsely and then winced and pressed his left palm into his ribs.

Cash met Alyssa's gaze. "Did he hit his head when he fell? Did he lose consciousness?"

"I'm not sure. Daddy?"

"I didn't knock myself out, if that's what you're asking. I'm pretty sure I didn't hit my head, but it happened so fast I can't be certain. I remember when I realized I was going to fall, I twisted to the side and tucked in my knees so I didn't land on my back."

"We can't be sure you didn't hit your head, then," Cash said. He nodded toward Alyssa. "You may be right about a possible concussion. Let me call Dr. Delia and see what she thinks about moving him."

Alyssa nodded gratefully.

Cash stepped out into the living room and called the town doctor, explaining the situation, asking whether they should move him or not and whether they'd made the right decision not to call 911.

Delia said she'd be right over and not to move Edward until she'd had the opportunity to check him out. If he needed to be transported to a hospital, she would call Ben and Zach, the local paramedics, from Edward's house.

"Dr. Delia's on her way," he said as he reentered the kitchen. Alyssa gave an audible sigh of relief as he knelt down beside her and brushed a reassuring hand across her shoulder. He wished he could do more.

"I trust Dr. Delia. She'll know what to do. I should have called her right away." She frowned and shook her head and her tears started again in earnest. "I'm just not thinking straight. I was going to ring Eddie, but then I realized he was out of cell phone range. Then for some reason you popped into my mind."

"Gee, thanks." He curled up one corner of his lips and winked at her.

She blushed. "That's not what I meant."

"No, I know." He brushed the wetness from her cheek with the tips of his fingers. "I'm just teasing you."

His gut clenched. Talk about feeling like a jerk. Now wasn't the time to be making jokes.

Within minutes, Delia arrived with her medical bag and checked out Edward, flashing a light into his eyes to examine his pupils and taking his blood pressure. She had him move his extremities and checked for broken bones.

Edward's hip hurt and his ribs were sore, but Delia said she suspected the pain came from the impact of the fall and not from any breaks or fractures.

Cash stood and stepped back, giving Delia room to move around the patient. He suddenly felt as if he didn't quite belong in this intimate family situation, seeing as he wasn't related to Edward and Alyssa.

He shoved his hands into the front pockets of his jeans and shifted from one foot to the other, wondering if he ought to just quietly let himself out. But then he thought about Alyssa.

She would need support after Delia left. He wasn't about to leave her alone when she might need him, so he leaned his hip against the counter near the stove, crossed his arms and watched from a distance.

When Delia had thoroughly examined Edward, she gave the go-ahead to move him into his bedroom. Cash and Alyssa braced the old man between them and slowly walked him down the hallway.

"No getting out of bed unless I say so," Alyssa warned her father as she tucked the covers under his chin.

Cash searched for the television remote and handed it to Edward.

"Could you please get him a glass of cold water?" Alyssa asked as she fussed over her father, plumping his pillows and adjusting them under his head.

"Sure thing."

As Cash entered the kitchen, Delia was just packing up the last of her supplies in her medical kit.

"When you and Alyssa are finished with Edward, I'd like to have a word with you both," Delia said.

Cash nodded and took the glass of cold water in to Edward, who was already drifting off to sleep.

Cash moved close to Alyssa and took her elbow. "Delia would like to speak to us."

"Us?" She raised her eyebrows.

"You. She wants to speak to you."

Delia had said she'd wanted to speak to them both, but she didn't have the full picture of why he was here. For all she knew, he was a dinner guest, instead of what had really happened, that Alyssa had phoned him out of sheer desperation when she'd found her father flat on the floor. If she'd had someone else to call, Cash figured she would have.

He placed his hand on the small of her back as they returned to the kitchen. Delia was already seated at the kitchen table and gestured for them each to take a seat. Alyssa flopped into a chair across from her, but Cash was too restless to sit.

"I don't think your dad has a concussion," Delia affirmed with a reassuring smile. "But he did take a hard fall, and he was already in a weakened state. Definitely keep a close eye on him for the next twenty-four hours. Have him remain in his bed as much as possible and be sure to give him a hand whenever he needs to walk, because his balance may be off for a while. I placed a lidocaine patch on his ribs and have prescribed some painkillers for his hip and back, which may leave him a bit dizzy and foggy-headed.

"Also, you can expect to see some fairly substantial bruising showing up in the next few days, particularly on his hip. If his symptoms get worse or he complains about something new, give me a call immediately."

"Will do," Cash said, moving to stand behind Alyssa's chair and laying his hands on her shoulders. He might technically be a third wheel, but knowing Edward, Alyssa was going to need all the help she could get to keep him in bed and resting. Granted, Alyssa had indicated that

Edward was already ill, but the man Cash remembered was a stubborn old goat. He'd be up and about far too soon if he wasn't being watched like a hawk.

Maybe he couldn't solve Alyssa's problems, exactly, but keeping Edward in bed, Cash could do.

Of course, Alyssa might not want him to stay. But he was going to offer—*insist*, for her own good. He was determined to be there for Edward.

For *her*.

Finding her father sprawled on the floor yesterday, howling in pain, had taken ten years off Alyssa's life. After dropping to his side to let him know she was there, she had immediately pulled out her cell phone to call for an ambulance, but her stubborn father hadn't let her.

So instead she'd called Cash.

Why *had* she called Cash?

It didn't make a lick of sense. He wasn't family. Though he was working at Emerson's he wasn't even a permanent employee. They weren't even close friends. Not really—or at least she hadn't thought of him that way until today.

Instead, it had been an instinctive gesture on her part. She'd desperately needed someone to be with her, to support her through this emergency, and with Eddie out on the range where he couldn't be reached, she didn't have any other family to turn to.

Even though her father hadn't wanted an ambulance, her first call should have been to the town doctor and she was annoyed and irritated with herself that it hadn't been. She couldn't believe she'd been so shaken that she hadn't even thought of that.

An ambulance, yes, but not Dr. Delia. Maybe it was because Alyssa knew Dr. Delia didn't usually work on Sundays, but she was always on call, so that was no excuse.

But Alyssa had been so frightened, had felt so helpless, that her brain was in a frenzy. With all the panic and adrenaline coursing through her, her mind had gone blank. It was all she could do to take in her father's condition and give him what comfort she could.

She'd pulled up her contact list and Cash's name had been near the top. The rest was instinct.

Cash's presence, oddly enough, had made her feel stronger, more capable and able to handle the crisis.

Thank the good Lord he'd also thought to phone Delia right away, allowing her to remain at her father's side while he spoke to the doctor.

Daddy hurting himself when she wasn't around to see it was exactly what she'd been afraid of ever since Mama had left them. Alyssa had her own apartment since she'd returned from getting her MBA and moved out of the family home.

Things had been fine back then. Her father had been an active man dedicated to making Emerson's Hardware all it could be. It had been Daddy's idea to contact Kickfire and he was the one who had originally planned the renovation—which was part of the reason Alyssa was so committed to seeing it through.

Deep in her heart, she hoped that maybe once the remodel was done, her father might see his way back to working in the store. That he might regain his strength. If she could provide him with a new purpose for his life, then maybe…

When Mama had taken off after Aaron's death, she had left her father all alone.

Alone, and now ill.

Alyssa would never get past her mother's betrayal. But she hoped her father would.

She'd believed that once he'd seen the work she'd done on the store renovation and the institution of the Kickfire brand, he would catch her enthusiasm and be anxious to return to work.

Now she wasn't so sure.

More than once since Mama had left, she'd considered moving back home to stay with Daddy and support him through what must certainly be the most difficult trial of his life, the abandonment by a life partner and the death of his son. But when she brought up the subject, Daddy had shot it down.

He didn't need help, he'd assured her. He was fine on his own.

But clearly, he wasn't fine, even if he was too stubborn to admit it.

Alyssa sighed and leaned into the cushion on the living room sofa, tilting her head back and closing her eyes. She was bone tired but too wound up to doze. The television was on, playing softly in the background, but she couldn't pay attention to whatever was on the screen.

It had been a close call today.

Much too close to ignore.

Things had to change, whether Daddy liked it or not. It was time to put her foot down. She didn't like telling her father what to do, but she and Eddie had some difficult decisions to make. At least she'd have her brother's support, so they would be able to present a united front when they laid down the new laws.

She sighed wearily. One thing was certain—Daddy could no longer live alone. Not in the state he was currently in. If it was purely grief, he wasn't coping well, and Alyssa wasn't sure he would ever fully recover. Not when he'd lost the will to try.

At the very least, Daddy was severely depressed. But if there was something medically wrong with him, she needed to know that, too. She would give Delia a call once this crisis had passed and ask her to give Daddy a thorough physical examination.

Alyssa yawned and glanced at her watch, then stood and stretched her arms over her head, bending her neck from side to side to remove the kinks.

It had been a long night that had morphed into an even longer day. She'd stopped by the store first thing in the morning and checked on the kittens, but then had left Emerson's closed for the day with a brief note taped to the window to explain.

Once her friends and neighbors in Serendipity heard what had happened, they would understand why she'd chosen to spend the day watching over her father. It wouldn't take long before her church family and neighborhood friends banded together to help care for her father.

Jo Spencer had already dropped by earlier in the morning with a care package, if one could call the entire passenger's seat of a pickup truck full of prepared food a "care package."

Casseroles, homemade soup, freshly baked bread and rolls, cookies, milk and butter—enough for her father to live on for at least a week, probably more.

Alyssa figured most of the food came from Jo's own café, Cup O' Jo's, but Jo must have raided Sam's Grocery, as well.

Presumably Jo had heard the news about Daddy from Dr. Delia. And if Jo knew, it wouldn't be long before the rest of the town found out what had happened.

Which was a good thing. Everyone close to Daddy, including Serendipity's local church, where he had attended regularly before Mama had left, would take it upon themselves to visit and make sure he was doing okay. Having folks who really cared about their neighbors was one of the biggest benefits of living in a small town where everyone knew each other.

It was past time for Alyssa to relieve Cash, who was sitting at Daddy's bedside, watching over him. When she'd left the two men, Cash had been reading the book *The Lord of the Rings* to him, which was one of Daddy's favorites. He was a big fan of fantasy novels.

Just after leaving the room earlier, Alyssa had hung around for a couple of minutes out of sight, listening to Cash read. He could have been an audiobook narrator, with his smooth, rich baritone voicing all the different characters. He even gave a couple characters a high, squeaky falsetto. She'd smiled softly before making her way out into the living room to crash on the couch for a while.

Despite her fatigue, she hadn't been able to doze as she'd hoped. The scene kept playing over and over in her mind. Daddy on the floor, helpless to get up on his own.

What if she hadn't been there? What if it hadn't been Sunday? What if he'd laid there for days instead of hours?

Shaking off her anxiety, she quietly walked to the hall that led to Daddy's room.

As tired and stressed out as everyone was, she expected to find Daddy sound asleep and Cash dozing in a chair by his bedside, the book propped open over his chest.

Instead, she found him halfway down the hallway, leaning his shoulder against the door frame of Aaron's old room, his lips pressed into a hard, straight line and his expression pensive as he stared into her brother's bedroom.

What was he doing in Aaron's room?

"Cash?" she murmured, placing a gentle hand on his shoulder.

He jerked as if jolted with a bolt of electricity and spun around, his eyes wide with shock. His breath came in heavy gasps as he ran his palm back through his hair, leaving the dark waves in unruly tufts and spikes.

He looked as if he'd seen a ghost.

"I'm sorry," she apologized, furrowing her brow. "I didn't mean to startle you."

"No. No." He blew out a breath. "It's okay. I was so lost in my thoughts I didn't hear you walk up."

"What are you doing?"

"Your dad is sound asleep. I doubt he'll wake for hours, but I didn't want to leave him until I knew you were awake to keep an eye on him."

"I'm glad to hear it. He needs his rest. But that wasn't what I asked."

She silently gestured toward Aaron's bedroom.

Cash glanced into Aaron's room again and his expression tightened with strain, so much so that Alyssa could see his pulse beating frantically in the corner of his jaw.

"I was coming out to see how you were faring, since I know what a stressful night it's been for you. I thought maybe you would have crashed on the couch. I planned to cover you up with a quilt and let you sleep for a while, since I'm wide-awake, anyway."

Alyssa's chest flooded with warmth. With all the rumors about Cash that were floating around before the day of the auction, she'd truly expected to find him no more than a callous cowboy who tromped his boots all over everyone to get what he wanted.

Instead, she saw before her a man with true compassion radiating from his azure eyes. Though he was thoroughly exhausted, she perceived sympathy in his gaze. He might have said he was wide-awake, but he certainly didn't look it.

He looked ready to drop, and Alyssa suspected that like her, he hadn't slept a wink, not even a light doze. And yet even so, he'd been ready and willing to take her shift, so she could get some sleep.

That wasn't the act of a heartless, insensitive man.

He was a complete enigma to her, that was for sure.

"The door was wide-open, and I couldn't help but notice it as I passed," Cash said, crossing his arms and leaning back against the wall. "I—I wasn't snooping."

She raised her brow. "I never said you were."

"I just—" He paused, his voice raspy. "I was surprised, that's all. Aaron's room hasn't changed a bit from when he was a teenager. We spent a lot of time in here, playing video games and hanging out together."

"I remember," she said softly. "My room was just

down the hall, and you two guys made quite a ruckus sometimes."

She didn't tell him that she'd always been especially mindful of him whenever he spent time with her brother. It was as if she had some kind of invisible connection to him whenever he was around.

He chuckled, but his amusement didn't reach his expression. "We were pretty rowdy, weren't we?"

She nodded. Their eyes met and held, and she could palpably feel his grief washing over him in great tidal waves.

"Daddy has kept Aaron's room like a shrine. I've tried to convince him that we need to go through Aaron's things eventually, even if Eddie and I are the ones doing it, but he won't hear of it."

She placed a hand over her rapidly beating heart, willing it to slow. Her chest contracted painfully.

"Unlike with Aaron, Daddy immediately wiped out every trace of my mother ever having lived here, but I think he's holding on to his memory of Aaron to get him through his own grief."

"I can't even imagine. What you and your family have been through—it's no wonder your father is having difficulty recovering from all the hardships he's been through recently. Any man would. But I can't express how sorry I am to see him this way."

That made two of them. It broke her heart every time she laid eyes on Daddy.

She was a little surprised that Cash realized the depth of her father's pain, and more than that, didn't think him weak for it.

"Is it okay if I—" He gestured, asking if he could enter the sanctuary of Aaron's room.

Alyssa nodded, tears pricking her eyes. She understood what Cash was asking. She'd spent a lot of time here in Aaron's room after he'd died, just sitting on his bed, sobbing quietly as she embraced her many happy memories of him.

His baseball trophies and the mitt and ball he'd used when the high school team had won the state championship when he was a senior were in a case along one wall. His favorite cartoon superhero posters lined his wall. In one corner lay stacks of rodeo magazines he'd collected as he'd dreamed about his future in pro rodeo.

Alyssa would never admit it to anyone, but sometimes she'd talk to Aaron—out loud, as if he was sitting there with her. She'd tell him about what was going on at the store, and how Eddie had found his calling as a wrangler.

Aaron would have liked that.

And sometimes, through her tears, she told him how much she loved him and missed him and how her life would never be the same without him.

Cash reached for the mitt and ball on the top of the display case, putting the mitt on his hand and tossing the ball in the air, easily catching it when it came down again. Cash had been a star first baseman during his high school years, but not as good as Aaron, who'd held the record for the number of strikes pitched, and who still held the school record to this day.

"If Aaron had lived in a bigger town, he could have gotten a full-ride scholarship to university," Cash said, his voice raspy and cracking with emotion. "He was that good."

Alyssa nodded.

Aaron had loved baseball and he *had* excelled in

it. But there'd always been something he'd loved even more.

"I don't think he would have taken a scholarship even if one had been offered to him," Alyssa said. "That wasn't his path. He would have been miserable in college. He never much cared for academics. All he ever really wanted to do was pro rodeo."

"He was good at that, too." One corner of Cash's lips curled up the faintest bit. "I was glad he was a saddle bronc rider and not bareback. We were always highly competitive with each other, even when we were kids, but I wouldn't have wanted to compete with him in the same rodeo event. As it was, we were both able to be the top dogs. It was much more fun that way."

He paused and coughed, as if to dislodge the emotions choking him. "At least it was, until—"

He paused.

"Oh, man." He grunted and squeezed his eyes closed, and for a moment Alyssa wondered if he was fighting back tears.

He cleared his throat again, shook his head and ran a hand down his face.

The effect was startling.

One second his expression had been full of sorrow and grief.

But when his eyes met hers for a second time, those emotions had morphed into something else entirely. To Alyssa's surprise, there was anger in his gaze, and his whole body tightened like a coiled spring. He looked like he was about to jump out of his skin.

What just happened?

"Cash?" she asked gently. She reached for his shoulder, but he jerked back, knocking her hand away.

"I can't do this," he ground out from between clenched teeth.

She didn't even have the opportunity to ask him what he meant before he stomped down the hallway at full stride and disappeared out of sight.

A moment later, she heard the front door slam shut.

She stared after him, her mouth agape. For some reason she couldn't begin to explain, she felt as if a door had slammed closed in her heart, as well.

Chapter Five

Unexpectedly discovering Aaron's bedroom looking just as it had been when Aaron was in high school had sucker punched Cash right in the gut.

The pain of seeing Aaron's things, looking as if they were waiting for their owner to come back and claim them, had been so acute that he'd quite literally lost his breath, and his chest had clenched so tightly it was as if his heart was being squeezed by a vise. His entire body screamed for the numbness a bottle of whiskey would provide.

He'd been downright rude to Alyssa when he'd left without an explanation, but he'd been choking in agony, and all he'd been able to think about at the time was getting as far away from the Emersons' home as possible, as fast as possible.

To be able to breathe again.

He felt horrible that he'd left Alyssa alone to deal with her father, that his own mortification had won out over his compassion for Alyssa and her father. It had taken him a whole week to feel as if he were back in Alyssa's good graces.

So much for the new moral code he was trying to establish. With that one act, he'd proven just exactly what kind of man he was, and he couldn't be more ashamed of his actions. He was weak and selfish.

Because he had taken off the way he did, Alyssa had no one else to spell her or give her a break.

Thankfully, Eddie had returned home Monday evening as he was supposed to do, and he'd helped Alyssa keep their stubborn father in bed to recuperate, but even that knowledge was little consolation to Cash.

The one good thing that had come out of it all was that Alyssa had once again invited Cash to church, and this time he'd agreed. It had taken seeing Aaron's bedroom to finally convince him he couldn't make it on his own.

As he stood by his truck in the parking lot of the church on a bright Sunday morning waiting for Alyssa to arrive, he nervously tapped his hat against his thigh and rubbed a hand across the tight muscles at the back of his neck. Even though he mentally coached himself to breathe normally, his breath was coming in short, shallow gasps.

Knowing he needed to get right with God and actually walking back into the sacred sanctuary of church were two different things entirely. And that was to say nothing about facing the community he'd rejected when he'd gone off on his own.

He'd interacted with friends and neighbors when they'd come into Emerson's, and like Nick and Slade McKenna, most of them had been friendly and accepting. He hoped that the church congregation would be equally as forgiving.

"Cash?" Alyssa reached out and shook his arm.

He looked at her, startled.

"I said your name twice," she explained, her lips curving up slightly. "You were way out there somewhere in the wild blue yonder."

He tried to smile.

"Just thinking."

She raised her brows. "About?"

He shook his head. "Nothing important."

She nodded toward the church building. "Are you ready to go?"

He tried to smile. "I guess so?"

The words came out as a question and Alyssa chuckled before tucking her hand through his arm.

"You'll be fine."

He wished he was as sure of himself as Alyssa appeared to be, but he had to admit it helped having her arm in his for support. Otherwise, he might have turned right around and gotten back in his truck.

"Eddie tried to coax Daddy into coming but he still refuses, so we won't have the wh—whole family here," she stammered.

She tensed, and he laid his hand on top of hers. It appeared they both needed support today.

His heart was slamming in his throat as they entered the sanctuary, but as they took their places beside Eddie and knelt for prayer before the service started, a sense of peace enveloped him.

He'd forgotten what it felt like to take time to focus on worshipping God—or maybe he'd never known. His mother had insisted on her only son attending the weekly service, and he'd seen her praying every night—probably for him. He'd dropped the habit of church worship the moment he'd left home, but he expected his mother still prayed for him nightly from her home in Scottsdale.

He finally understood what his mother had tried so hard to teach him.

He felt the presence of God.

"Why do you think Jesus used sheep to represent us in his parables?" Pastor Shawn asked during the homily. "Why not wolves? Or sharks?"

Because I'm as stupid as a sheep, Cash thought, slinking down in the pew and crossing his arms. Following the crowd into sin and error without a second thought.

"Because the sheep is the strongest of all animals," the pastor continued with a knowing grin.

For a man who ministered in a small ranching town like Serendipity, Pastor Shawn had certainly missed the mark with that statement. Had he ever even been to Rowdy Masterson's sheep farm and seen sheep in action?

"Why are the sheep strong? Because they are cared for by the Good Shepherd. He puts a fence around them, keeps the wolves at bay. Look to Jesus, for it is through Him that we become strong. God puts a fence around us to keep us safe and makes our community a family."

Cash was floored at the way Pastor Shawn had flipped the well-known parable on its head. And it made so much sense.

Following all his newly implemented moral principles meant nothing without a real relationship with Jesus and the Christian community.

His strength didn't come from himself. God was his strength. And his church family was his home.

* * *

With this realization fresh in his heart, he was a little nervous going into the fellowship hall after the service. Practically everyone he knew milled about somewhere in that room, enjoying coffee and doughnuts and a chance to catch up.

The question was, would they want to catch up with *him*?

He shouldn't have worried. Jo Spencer was the first to approach him, giving him a boisterous hug and loudly proclaiming how happy she was to see him back at the Lord's house.

As he sipped on his coffee and scarfed down his doughnut, he was surrounded by his old ranching buddies, and before long, they were laughing and joking as if Cash had never been gone.

As if he hadn't ruined his life.

Gruff Frank Spencer, Jo's husband, slapped his back in greeting and asked if they could take a walk.

Curious, Cash agreed.

"Look," Frank said when they were beyond the earshot of the folks in the fellowship hall. "I've never been one to beat around the bush, so I'm just gonna say it. You're an alcoholic. That will never be past tense. And it's not something you can do alone."

Just when Cash had started relaxing, he got hit with this. Was Frank judging him here?

"I know," Frank said, and Cash's gut turned over. "Because I'm a recovering alcoholic myself."

Frank Spencer? Head of the town council? A recovering alcoholic?

He made no excuses. Just told it like it was. Cash had to admire that in a man.

"Now, look. Jo told me you ain't going to meetings."

Cash nodded. "That's not my thing."

"Well, it ought to be."

"Sorry. I don't think so. It's my problem and I have to deal with it."

"Son, you're making a mistake."

Cash shrugged. He didn't want to argue with the old man.

Frank pulled out his wallet and handed Cash a card.

"Well, if you ain't gonna take my advice, then at least take my number. Call me anytime, day or night. Deal?"

"Yes, sir," Cash agreed, pocketing the card. He'd never use it, but it was nice of Frank to put himself out there this way. The man didn't parade his alcoholism in front of the world. Cash certainly never would have guessed.

Frank was a role model in that way. If he could do it, Cash could, too. Get beyond the label and move on with his life.

Move on with his life.

Alyssa's face immediately popped into his mind. He was attracted to her, no doubt about that. But could moving on with his life include a relationship? Something long-term and meaningful?

That was a stretch. At least right now, it was. Even after giving God the reins in his life, he still knew he had a long way to go.

But maybe someday he could stoke the fire between him and his pretty boss.

She'd invited him to the family dinner this afternoon.

That was as good a place as any to start.

Alyssa fussed about as she laid the place settings on her father's dining room table. It had been a long-standing family tradition to get together for Sunday dinner, for as far back in Alyssa's childhood as she could remember.

After her mother left, that tradition had dropped by the wayside. It was only recently that Alyssa had brought what was left of the family back together to share a meal once a week and catch up on all that was happening with each other.

Today was different. It was silly of her to be making such a big deal over the table settings, but she wanted it to be perfect. She'd even laid out their nicest porcelain plates and crystal glasses for her homemade lemonade.

Cash was joining them for dinner today. Why that should make such a big difference was beyond her, but she couldn't seem to coax her pulse into anything close to its normal rate.

Family dinners already felt strained with its missing members—Mom at the foot of the table and Aaron sitting next to Eddie. Those two boys could never keep their hands off each other and were always pushing and elbowing each other.

These days Eddie just scarfed his food and made his excuses.

When she heard a knock at the front door, she knew it was Cash, since Eddie just let himself into their childhood home. She went to the door and greeted her guest.

He had one arm behind his back, and with a big smile, he presented her with a bouquet of colorful wildflowers native to Texas.

"For you."

"Thank you," she replied in a hoarse whisper. "They're beautiful."

Well, this was unexpected. He'd said the flowers

were for her, but he probably meant for the family, as a centerpiece. Didn't he?

"Come on in."

Eddie was on the couch playing a video game and offered Cash a controller. Within moments the two men were vying for a position on the driving game they were playing.

"I'll just put these in a vase," she said to no one in particular. "They'll make a wonderful centerpiece."

After taking care of the flowers, she went to check on her father. She was surprised to find he was already up, showered and shaved and was running a comb back through his mad-scientist hair.

Since Eddie had indicated her father still wasn't ready to return to church, she hadn't realized the extent of his improvement.

"Daddy?"

He met her with a smile.

"You look—" She was so choked up she couldn't find the words.

His gray eyes glittered with amusement, something she hadn't seen in oh, so long.

"Handsome?" he supplied for her. "Dashing?"

She giggled. "Cash is here. Are you about ready to eat?"

He patted his too-thin stomach. "I could eat a horse."

"We're having chicken. I hope that's okay," she joked back, her joy at seeing her father up and about bubbling over into her words.

"Fried chicken?"

"Of course."

"Homemade?"

Alyssa burst out laughing. "No such luck. You know

I don't have time to cook. I picked up a chicken from Sam's Grocery yesterday along with all the fixings and one of Phoebe Hawkins's cherry pies for dessert."

Phoebe worked at Jo's café and was known far and wide for her delicious pastries.

Tossing his comb on the bathroom counter, her father slung a bony arm around her shoulder and suggested they go find "the boys."

His statement was so close—almost—to what once had been, and once again Alyssa got choked up, although now for another reason.

The boys used to be Eddie and Aaron.

Now Aaron was gone, and Cash was here. Life would certainly never be the same, but for maybe the first time since Aaron's death, Alyssa could picture a future, could see herself moving forward.

With Cash?

As Cash and the family chatted over dinner, Alyssa considered that thought. Cash fit in well, giving as much as he took, laughing and joking.

"So what do you think, Edward?" Cash said after dinner was finished and Cash had helped Alyssa clear the table. Eddie had returned to his video game, but Cash lingered near the dining room. "Are you up for a game of chess?"

If Alyssa was worried that it might be too much for her father, she shouldn't have been. Edward wiped the board with Cash—and Alyssa didn't think he let the old man win, either.

Score one for Daddy.

"Do you miss working at the shop? Do you want to come back?" Cash asked as he set up the pieces for a second game.

Alyssa's heart just about stopped at Cash's forward questions. Just laying it right out on the line.

They appeared to take her father by surprise, as well, and no wonder. He ran a hand through his hair, returning it to its usual scraggly peaks, and stared at Cash with wide eyes.

"Maybe soon. I'd like to," he said tentatively. "I don't know. I'm not ready yet."

"It's okay, sir," Cash assured him. "Alyssa and I have everything under control. I just wanted you to know we'll welcome you back whenever you're ready."

Her father beamed from ear to ear. His face was quite literally glowing. He almost looked healthy.

All because of Cash. It hadn't escaped Alyssa's notice that Cash had taken ownership of the store, made it sound as if he was a part of it.

And he was, she realized with a start. He'd weaved himself into the day-to-day doings of the shop, become an invaluable part of what made Emerson's thrive. Watching him move heavy feed sacks like they weighed nothing, his biceps bulging with the effort. Seeing him fronting product with Maus on his shoulder purring contentedly. Cash standing behind the register helping a little old lady feel like she was the most important person in the world.

When he left, he'd be leaving a gaping hole.

And as for Alyssa, well, she'd miss him, too. Probably much more than she should.

His thoughtfulness. His friendship. A crooked grin that did funny things to her insides, and that charming Texas drawl that melted her bones.

Yes, if she was being honest, the real hole would be left in her heart.

Chapter Six

❧

The next few months working at the store had been crazy busy most of the time. Alyssa walked around in a daze, stressed and exhausted.

Cash took on more responsibility than ever, trying to pick up the slack and relieve Alyssa of some of her burden.

He'd even accompanied her to see Edward a few times. The old man was looking better, but he was nowhere near healed.

When Cash reached the store on an overcast Tuesday morning in early November, he was surprised to find that Alyssa was already there, checking the contents of boxes littered all over the floor, rearranging them into multicolored plastic bins and making notes on a yellow legal pad attached to a clipboard.

As if it wasn't odd enough that the front of the store was strewn with boxes at this early hour, the crates were full to brimming of food—the one thing catchall Emerson's Hardware *didn't* sell. Turkeys, hams, boxes of stuffing mix, bags of potatoes, frozen broccoli, fresh bread.

"Let me guess," he said, picking up a box of brownie mix. "You are going to be cooking the biggest Thanksgiving feast ever in the history of mankind."

She grinned. "Something like that."

He raised a brow.

"Can I use your truck?"

"Only if you tell me what you're really doing."

"What *we're* doing, you mean."

"O-kay." He drew out the word.

"All of this food is for charity. You know the reminder the pastor gave us about a food drive? We've been collecting items at church and keeping them in the church storage room for a couple of weeks now—with the obvious exception of the fresh foods, which were donated by Sam's Grocery and Cup O' Jo's Café. I picked all those up this morning. We need to get this food separated and boxed up into Thanksgiving meals and then we'll take the bins to some families who are running a little short this year."

"And you want me to help?" His heart warmed. Martin had been pushing him to do charitable works but all Cash ever wanted to do was say no. It didn't seem right, somehow, to pretend as someone who cared about people, when really, all he'd ever cared about was himself.

But when Alyssa presented him with this opportunity, it was a whole other thing.

"Only if you want to," she qualified.

"Of course he wants to." Martin's voice came from the front of the store, making Cash cringe. He hadn't bothered locking the door when he'd entered, since he'd assumed they'd be open for business within the hour. "This is a perfect photo op. Brilliant. I don't know why

I didn't think of it myself. Cash feeding the poor. Let's not rush things. I'm getting on the phone with Pete right now. He's in town for a few days anyway doing a shoot on the Second Chance Ranch Horse Challenge. I know he'll want to document this. It'll only take him a minute to get over here."

Cash's gaze flashed back to Alyssa. She was staring at Martin as if he'd just suggested eating worms for breakfast. Her face flushed an angry red as her eyes met Cash's.

"I need something out of the storage room," she stated, turning away from him and stalking toward the back. "Cash, can you help me?"

She didn't even wait to see if he was following her, but the moment they were alone, she rounded on him like a cornered tiger.

"I'm sorry, but I've had quite enough of you being photographed or filmed every time you do something nice for someone. It's all fake and I don't like it. Doesn't that bother you even just a little bit?"

More than she would ever know.

He wished he'd never brought Martin and Pete into Alyssa's life. She had more than enough to deal with, without his agent poking his nose into her business.

"I have an idea," he said, putting his arm around her shoulder and leaning in conspiratorially. "A way we can salvage this situation."

"Let's hear it."

"Why don't we finish organizing and go ahead and load up the food into my truck as we'd planned. Act as if we've agreed to the photo op. Then we make a run for it. Lose 'em."

"Seriously?"

"You bet. It'll be fun. No doubt they'll try to follow us, but I think with effort we can give them the slip. Get them all turned around before we head where we're really going."

"Like in the movies?"

"Exactly."

"I don't know how effective that will be, given how small Serendipity is. They're bound to catch up with us sooner or later. All they have to do is keep driving around. But I suppose that will at least give us the opportunity to deliver some of the care packages."

"If we can ditch them once, we can do it again, until our work is accomplished."

She chuckled. "That's the name of the game."

"What? Ditch?"

"Ding-dong ditch, to be precise. Did you ever play that game when you were a kid? Ring someone's doorbell and then run away and hide before they caught you?"

"I had a few dozen girlfriends in high school." He pressed out his chest like a rooster and chuckled. "I was the one getting my doorbell rung at all hours of the day and night—which annoyed my parents to no end."

"Braggart."

"Just telling it like it is."

"I'm sure." She rolled her eyes. "Now, let's finish sorting through the food and load it up on your truck."

"We can ask Martin and Pete to help with organizing the food. I'm not sure about Martin, but I think we can enlist Pete."

He started to head out of the storeroom when Alyssa caught his arm.

He turned and questioned her with a look.

"You're sure you don't want to make this into a promo op? It would look good on your résumé."

Cash knew what it took for her to ask that question and he appreciated the sacrifice, but this project was a real act of community charity. If everyone knew he'd participated, what was the point?

"I'm positive," he assured her. "Now let's get this stuff loaded up and get out of here."

Though they'd grown closer over time and Alyssa knew Cash had a kind heart beating in that big ol' chest of his, she was still taken by surprise when he'd so easily dropped what would have been the perfect photo op.

This could have turned out to be a disaster, but Cash was turning it into something exciting. The last thing she wanted to do was have Pete following them around snapping pictures. It would take all the fun out of the day.

But she wasn't sure it was fair to him. Cash had given her far more than she'd ever expected when she'd bid on him at the auction, and she wanted to make sure he got what he needed to clean up his image and return to rodeo.

And he *would* return to his high-adrenaline lifestyle, probably sooner rather than later. He never complained about his current lifestyle but keeping shop with her couldn't possibly be enough for a man like Cash.

Her chest squeezed tight around her heart when she thought about him leaving. There had never been any question of that being the end goal, and yet it was hard to imagine going back to the solitary existence she'd lived before he'd come along.

Could she run Emerson's by herself?

Of course she could. She'd done it before. She could do it again.

But it would never be the same. There would always be something—some*one*—missing.

"We're all loaded up," Cash said, leaning down to whisper in her ear. "Are you ready to lose the extra weight?"

She giggled. She had to admit, this was going to be fun. Cash certainly livened up her life.

"On the count of three, then," he continued in a soft, husky voice. "Hop into the truck and we'll peel on out of here."

She nodded.

He grinned. "One...two...*three*."

He grabbed her hand and they raced for his truck. By the time she'd thrown herself into the passenger side of the cab and slammed the door shut behind her, Cash had already revved up the engine and put the truck into gear. As he'd promised, he peeled off down the street, the wheels screeching as he turned a tight corner.

Alyssa looked back just in time to see Martin and Pete standing on the sidewalk in front of the store, their mouths gaping open and stunned expressions on their faces.

"Ha. We did it," she cheered.

"You didn't think we would? I'm offended that you doubted me."

She laughed. "Oh, I didn't. Not for one second. Now, here comes the really fun part."

"I thought getting rid of Martin and Pete was the fun part."

"Your day is only starting. Do you remember where Cliff Johnson and his family live?"

"Still in that housing community out past the park?"

"Yep. Cliff fell ill recently and wasn't able to wrangle cows for a few months. He was in the hospital and now they're coping with a ton of medical bills. And as if that wasn't enough, they have a baby to look out for. It's been rough on the whole family. The holidays are going to be tough on them this year."

"And now we're bringing them Thanksgiving dinner. Do they attend church?"

"Oh, no. At least, not for years."

"That's a really cool thing for you to do for them."

Her gaze widened. "Oh, it's not just me. Many fellow parishioners helped gather everything. We have a food drive going year-round not only for the food bank but especially in preparation for the holidays."

He flashed a glance at her. "Just how early did you show up this morning to organize all the food into bins?"

"Oh-dark-thirty. I think I started at about 3:00 a.m."

"Why didn't you call me?"

"Let's see…because it *was* three o'clock in the morning and most people are sleeping?"

"I would have come, you know. To help you. We could have gotten the work done in half the time."

She chuckled. "Well, I'll know for next time."

Except there wouldn't be any next time. Cash would be gone long before she would be delivering food again just before Christmas.

Cash pulled his truck onto the Johnsons' street and started to park in front of the house.

"No, wait," Alyssa exclaimed, reaching for his arm. "Ding-dong ditch, remember? This is supposed to be anonymous. Park the truck around the corner."

"Oh, yeah. Right." Blue eyes gleamed with the thrill of adventure as he pulled the truck around the corner and put it in Park.

Cash unloaded a bin from the back of his truck and turned to Alyssa.

"Lead the way."

"We have to be super quiet and sneaky." Her gaze narrowed on him and she pursed her lips. "How are we going to do this with you carrying such a heavy bin?"

His laugh rent the air and he looked immediately repentant.

"Honey," he said in an exaggerated whisper, bobbing his eyebrows for emphasis, "have you ever picked up a hay bale? Way, way heavier than any of these bins, and I regularly tote two at a time."

She clapped a hand over her mouth to stifle the chuckle that left her lips.

"Okay, then, Hercules, we need to keep our heads low, so they don't see us if they happen to look out the front window. We'll tiptoe up to the porch and drop the food off in front of their door."

"And then ring the doorbell and run like crazy," Cash finished for her.

She could tell he was enjoying this. She was enjoying this—more than she had in the past. Something about sharing the moment with Cash made it extra special.

Continuing to laugh quietly under her breath, she followed Cash to the front of the house and helped him gently release the crate onto the wooden porch. She winced when the bin thumped against a loose board and they both froze where they were.

"Go ring the doorbell," he whispered.

"No. This is your first time playing the game. You do it."

He looked like he was ready to argue the point, but then he shrugged and flashed her a toothy grin.

"Ready?" He hovered his finger just above the doorbell.

She nodded vigorously, already half stepping off the porch.

Cash punched the doorbell multiple times, gave a quiet whoop and jumped off the porch, missing the stairs entirely. He reached for her hand as they dove for the hedge of evergreen shrubs near the side of the house.

A branch scratched her forearm, drawing tiny rivulets of blood, but she didn't care. She couldn't feel a thing with the amount of adrenaline pumping through her plus Cash's hand linked with hers.

She started giggling. Cash gently clamped his hand over her mouth as the door opened and Cliff Johnson stepped out onto the porch, dressed in tattered jeans and a white T-shirt, his feet bare.

His eyes widened when he saw the bin of food and he looked around, gazing up and down the street in search of a vehicle. Alyssa froze, not even daring to breathe. The whole point of this game was not to get caught.

"Teresa, come out here," Cliff called. A moment later his wife appeared on the doorstep, carrying their nine-month-old baby boy on her hip.

"What is it?"

Cliff pointed at the plastic bin. "A blessing."

Tears welled in Teresa's eyes. "Who from?"

"I don't know. They disappeared before I got to the

door and there doesn't appear to be a note. I think they must want to remain anonymous."

"Well, God knows who they are and how much this means to us. Lord bless them."

Cliff agreed and bent down to pick up the bin. Teresa held the screen door for him while he toted it inside.

Cash and Alyssa remained crouched behind the bush until Teresa closed the door and a few more minutes had passed. Then Cash stood and offered his hand to Alyssa to help her up.

"We'd better get out of here before they decide to take a second look around and catch us," she said. He'd kept her hand in his and they walked together back to the truck. It felt right, somehow, as they shared this special moment together.

"What Teresa said back there?" Cash said, a catch in his throat. "We've been blessed, all right. I've always been a taker, not a giver. I could get used to this feeling. I've never experienced anything quite like it."

"I'm sure it's much different than the rush you get from bareback bronc riding, but it really gets your heart beating, doesn't it?"

"I don't know about you, but I need all the blessings I can get," Cash said, nodding. "There are quite a few bins left in the back of the truck. We'd best get busy and start passing those mutual blessings around."

Chapter Seven

Cash had woken up earlier than usual and decided to head straight to the shop, thinking to get a head start on the day before Alyssa got there.

Their charity ding-dong ditch had given him a lot to think about. He wasn't sure when, but somewhere along the way since he'd returned to Serendipity, his focus had gone from his selfish needs and problems to how to help others, whether it was delivering Thanksgiving dinners to needy families or working behind the scenes to make Alyssa's load lighter at the store.

There was one part of his life that wasn't even close to coming together for him, and he'd been mulling over it for weeks.

His life was a lot different now.

He was a lot different.

He hadn't had a good night's sleep in ages because he couldn't stop thinking of what he hadn't put right. What he wanted more than life itself.

His *baby*.

The more time that passed, the more certain he was that he wanted—*needed*—to be a part of his baby's life. Not just on the outside looking in, offering child support and nothing more, but being a real, live, active parent. He was tired of waiting on Sharee to make all the decisions regarding their child. He wanted shared custody.

He was pulled from his thoughts when Alyssa arrived. If she was surprised that Cash had arrived early for work, she didn't comment on it. Cash folded T-shirts and placed them on a table by color and size.

Alyssa usually chattered as she worked, telling him stories about her childhood or the latest town gossip. But she appeared to have picked up on Cash's subdued mood and silently wandered around the store fronting product and making notes on where she needed to restock.

He didn't mean to be rude, but he was well aware he might be coming off that way. He didn't want to hurt her feelings, but he couldn't unravel all the thoughts in his head, much less talk about them. And his head was screaming for a drink. He could barely get past that ache to think about anything else.

It was a good fifteen minutes before Alyssa finally spoke to him.

"We got in a delivery of feed this morning," she informed him, her gaze curious and her voice a quiet monotone that didn't give away her feelings one way or the other. "There are four pallets out in the alley that need to be unloaded and placed in the back room. Check the front first to see if you need to restock. I think the chicken feed is low."

"Yes, ma'am." It was all he could think of to say, but he knew he needed to speak up. The unnatural quiet between them was nearly palpable.

"Alyssa, I—" He paused and cleared his throat, not sure how to go on.

With a pair of boots in her hand, Alyssa turned around and leaned her hip against the wooden boot display, giving him her full attention.

"Yes?" she asked when he didn't continue.

I—what?

I'm sorry because I can't figure out my own mind, much less speak it?

He grunted and shook his head. Breaking his gaze away from hers, he strode past her and into the back room. There were pallets waiting for him to unload.

Might as well get to work. He obviously wasn't going to solve anything with words.

Anxiety repeatedly stung him like a swarm of angry wasps as he threw fifty-pound bags of feed over his shoulders and carried them two at a time into the back room, slinging them down into messy piles on the floor with more force than was strictly necessary. He'd organize them later.

He kept his mind on his work. At least the heavy labor took most of his concentration. His muscles burned with the effort. It was just what he needed right now.

Cash was almost finished unloading the last pallet when Alyssa entered the stockroom. She didn't say a word, just slipped behind the oak desk she used to do the accounting and tucked herself into her oversize office chair.

He could feel her eyes on him. It made him itchy all over and he barely resisted the urge to scratch.

"Cash?" she said at last. "Will you please join me here at the desk for a moment?"

Cash swept his hat from his head and curled the brim in his fist as he approached. She gestured to the chair opposite her, but he shook his head, preferring to stand.

"You're making me nervous stalking back and forth like a caged lion," Alyssa said. "Sit."

Cash sat.

She hadn't barked out the command as she would have had he been a badly behaved dog or something, but that was how he felt. He tossed his hat onto the desk and crossed his arms over his chest in an instinctively defensive gesture.

Which was hardly fair. If anything, given his attitude this morning, she ought to be the one on the offensive. Yet he didn't sense that from her. He didn't know what she was thinking.

She stared at him, unblinking, unsettling him. Stoked heat flamed into a bonfire in his chest and rose to his face. The woman had the power to unnerve him more than anyone he'd ever known.

He'd always been so confident. So self-assured—especially with women. He hadn't bothered to think or care much about how others felt, as long as he got his way. Even as an adult, he'd been incredibly immature in both his thoughts and his actions. Shame filled him whenever he thought about it, which, given that he would soon be a father, was often.

Suddenly it mattered what other people thought of him—what *Alyssa* thought of him. He was walking on eggshells and he didn't like the way that made him feel.

He slid a quick glance at her to see if he could read her expression. He'd meant to look away again, but she caught his gaze and locked it with hers.

Her brow furrowed, but it wasn't a frown.

She was concerned—about *him*.

He wasn't used to that. The people he used to hang around only wanted him for what he could give them, just as he was only interested in taking what he wanted.

"What can I do for you?" she asked softly.

He choked on his breath and couldn't force air back into his lungs to save his life.

Alyssa wasn't taking.

She was *giving*.

"Look. I know something is bothering you. It's your choice whether or not you want to share it with me, of course, but I'm warning you now, that if you don't, my overactive imagination is going to come up with way worse scenarios than whatever your reality happens to be."

"I highly doubt that."

There was nothing worse than his reality.

"Is Martin breathing down your neck?"

He scoffed. "Martin is always breathing down my neck. Nothing new about that."

"And Pete?"

"Well, I don't know the guy from Adam. I don't particularly like him sticking a camera in my face every two seconds and I'm glad he's found other things to do than trailing behind me like a lost puppy all the time, but he's doing what Martin paid him to do, and he seems like a nice enough guy. Can't blame him for that."

"So, not Martin, and not Pete."

Cash shook his head.

"Are you worried about your baby?" Her voice had dropped to a faint whisper and he had to lean toward her to make out her words. "Have you gotten anywhere with Sharee at all, or is she still refusing to speak to you?"

He pressed his lips together to keep from saying just exactly what he thought of Sharee's fortification tactics. Alyssa already knew everything there was to know.

He'd never had trouble with his emotions before. He was about as far from being a sensitive guy as east was from west. The media, though admitting to his supposed charm and proven abilities in the rodeo arena, had labeled him cold and callous, and he'd always assumed they were right.

After Aaron's death, he'd gone from carefree to overwhelmed with guilt, so he'd drowned his thoughts and numbed his emotions with alcohol instead of letting himself feel things.

Even now, sitting across from a woman who truly cared about him, he experienced the urge to drink. It was an easy way out of dealing with his problems, but far from a simple one. Yet both his throat and his heart ached for the burn of whiskey to take the edge off his pain.

He didn't know how Alyssa did it—kept going in the wake of her brother's death, her mother's abandonment and her father's health issues, much less keeping the store running as successfully as she had.

He was barely able to cope with his best friend in heaven, his pro rodeo career in tatters and, most important, a baby on the way whose mother wanted nothing to do with him.

"Is Sharee finally starting to come around to see your side of things?" she prompted when he didn't im-

mediately answer her question. "You are the baby's father and have as many rights to that child as she has."

"No. I haven't heard a single word from her. I've
called her numerous times, but she always sends me to
voice mail. Honestly, I don't think she's ever going to
acknowledge my rights as a father to our baby."

"That isn't her choice to make. Maybe it's time to
confront her face-to-face. The longer you wait, the
harder it's going to get between the two of you."

He blew out a breath. "You're right. Whether she
likes it or not, Sharee and I are permanently connected
through this child. It's essential for me to convince her
of that. The sooner the better. We have a lot of details
to work out."

"I'm sorry. I wouldn't want to be in your place."

He clamped his jaw around the surge of anger he
felt, directed at the one person entirely responsible for
the trouble he was in.

Himself.

"I dug my own hole, and I'm the one responsible for
getting myself out of it," he acknowledged. "Just because I was under the influence of alcohol at the time
and didn't think my actions through to their logical
conclusions aren't acceptable excuses. I was young
and stupid enough to believe I was invincible. I didn't
think the rules of the natural order applied to me. And
then my whole world blew up in my face."

"It must have been a pretty big shock to discover you
had a baby on the way." If it had been anyone else, her
words might have sounded like an accusation, but with
Alyssa, it was commiseration mixed with sympathy.

"You can say that again. I can't believe I had to find
out I was going to be a father while watching the news

on television. I felt like someone had pulled the rug right out from under me."

He ran his palm across his whiskered jaw and caught Alyssa's gaze. "But can I tell you something I've never admitted to anyone before?"

Her eyes widened, and she gave him the slightest nod, so tiny he almost missed it.

"That very first moment when I found out I was going to be a father, when I saw the original ultrasound picture of my baby flashing across the television screen—well, everyone expected that my initial reaction would be denial. That I'd be angry at Sharee for putting the news on television before I even knew of my baby's existence. Which of course I was, and am."

"She should have told you first before making it public."

"Yes. She should have. But you know what? Even finding out the way I did, standing in the middle of a bar, half-drunk and with every single aspect of my life headed straight down into a pit of fire, my very first reaction when I saw my baby was—"

He was so choked up he could barely speak. He searched his mind for a way to explain his emotions.

"I'm not even sure I have the right word for it."

She smiled gently, patiently waiting for him to finish his sentence.

He placed his hand over his heart.

"Joy? Amazement? Downright wonder? All of the above, and then some?"

"You're going to be a daddy."

"Exactly."

How was it that Alyssa could understand what was

in his heart, when he barely knew it himself? And yet he could tell by her warmhearted gaze that she did.

"I know I don't deserve it. The way my child was conceived wasn't just a mistake, or something I can write off because I was too drunk to know my own actions.

"It was sin. I've always known the difference between right and wrong, even when I refused to admit it. I learned it in church and on my own daddy's knee. I knew what God expected me to do—and not do—and I chose to ignore Him. And I'm not proud of the kind of man that makes me."

He didn't give her the opportunity to interrupt, suspecting that she would probably try to take the heat off him. He didn't want the heat off him.

He deserved to be scorched.

"But this baby?" he continued, surprising himself by the smile that slightly curved his lips in an upward slope. "My son or daughter is a blessing, and I downright refuse to look at him or her any other way."

"I can't say how much I respect you for saying that. There are many men who wouldn't."

"I'm not most men."

No. He wasn't. He was scraping the bottom of the barrel.

But at least he was trying to climb out of it. And even in his foolishness, he could recognize the hand of God, forming a tiny human in a mother's womb, as something amazing and wondrous.

Alyssa said she respected him for his decision. Somehow, that made a difference, and when he stood up and grabbed his hat off the desk, planting it firmly on his head and adjusting the brim, he stood a bit taller, his shoulders a little straighter.

"Is there anything else you wanted to speak to me about?" He didn't want to look as if he was trying to rush off, but in truth he was.

"I suppose not," she said tentatively, brushing a stray strawberry-blond curl behind her ear. Her expression clearly indicated that she didn't feel they'd reached any kind of resolution, and she was right, but that would have to wait.

"Is it okay if I take a break?" he asked. "I have something I need to do real fast."

"Sure. No problem. You can finish stocking the feed up front when you return."

"Will do," he said, grinning and tipping his hat at her. "And thanks."

She tilted her head up at him, her gaze questioning. "For what?"

"For listening."

And for reminding him what was truly important in his life.

Not Martin, for all his blustering, or Pete trying to photograph Cash in the best light, or anything else having to do with this ridiculous publicity scheme.

Not even his rodeo career, as much as he intended to eventually return to the circuit. He needed to be successful now, more than ever, because he would soon have a child to support.

He exited the store and half jogged to his truck, fishing his cell phone out of his pocket as he went.

Once he'd settled himself behind the wheel and tossed his hat onto the passenger seat, he unlocked the phone screen and checked his contact list, taking a deep, stabilizing breath before punching the call button.

This was it. No holds barred. If he had to, he was

going to call over and over until she picked up her phone just to get him to stop.

The phone rang four and then five times before going to Sharee's voice mail. Cash closed the call and redialed.

Still no answer.

He hung up and dialed yet again, determined not to let her off the hook without speaking to her.

He tried two more times, growing more frustrated by the minute.

He almost dropped the phone in surprise when Sharee suddenly picked up on the sixth try.

"Hello?" The word came out half a yawn and very groggy sounding, and he suspected that even though it was half past three in the afternoon on a weekday, he'd woken her up, which was possibly why she'd answered the phone at all. Maybe she hadn't even bothered looking at the caller ID.

Finally, a little bit of luck. No—not luck. God was in this.

"Hello, Sharee," he said before she could hang up on him. "It's Cash."

"Cash?" she mumbled, as if she didn't quite place the name.

"We need to talk. About our baby."

"What?" She apparently bumped the phone with her chin as she shifted, and Cash heard a man's low groan in the background.

Something about hearing that sound made him furious.

It wasn't jealousy. He'd never cared for Sharee, not in the way that a man should care for a woman in such intimate circumstances.

He barely knew her. But he did know enough to suspect this man wasn't her boyfriend, any more than Cash had been. He was probably some rodeo cowboy she'd picked up in the bar and taken home with her.

Just as she'd done with him.

He prayed that she had changed, that instead of moving from one man to the next, she'd found someone with whom she could experience a healthy relationship; a man who would marry her, watch out for her and protect her—and their baby.

This time it *was* jealousy that surged through him. *He* was the baby's father. He and Sharee might end up co-parenting, but that child would know their real father's love.

"What do you want, Cash?" Sharee asked, her voice raspy from sleep.

"I was calling to see when it would be convenient to meet up with you face-to-face. I'd like to connect as soon as possible. We have a lot of details to work out between us regarding how we are going to care for our baby."

Sharee offered nothing more than a stunned silence on the other end of the line. He could hear her breathing, but that was all.

"For starters," he continued, "you don't have to worry that I might not pay child support, because I will, and on time, too. There's no question about that. I want our baby to have the best of everything."

"Stop right there, Cash. That's not going to be an issue, so you don't have to worry about it."

He wasn't worrying—he was just letting her know he was stepping up.

"You don't understand. I'm telling you I want to contribute to our baby's welfare. Be a real father."

"No, *you* don't understand. You won't be losing any of your hard-earned rodeo money paying child support."

There was a brusque tone to her voice that concerned Cash nearly as much as her words did. They were talking about their baby, here. Of course he was going to contribute.

"What?" He threaded his fingers through his hair. "What's that supposed to mean?"

Why wasn't she getting that he didn't give a fig about the money? It almost sounded as if she intended to provide for the baby on her own.

Which wasn't going to happen. This was all about his *child*, a baby he had already, in some inexplicable way, come to love, and was unquestionably responsible to care for.

"What that means, *Cash*," she said, overemphasizing his name, "is there is no baby."

She paused long enough for Cash to feel like he'd just been T-boned by a semitruck.

Tears burned in his eyes and his gut churned. He thought he was going to be sick.

"Did you—did our baby—"

"Take a breath. That wasn't what I meant. The baby is fine."

The relief that flooded over him made him feel like his bones had suddenly turned into jelly. He slumped over the wheel, allowing his tears to fall unheeded onto his black T-shirt.

With every part of his being, he struggled to compose himself and not come completely unglued. For that one awful moment when he thought his baby was gone…

He hadn't realized until he thought that he had lost his baby how much he really *did* want his child.

Thank God. Oh, thank God. It was as much of a prayer as he could offer through his clouded thoughts.

The baby was safe.

His baby was safe.

Had Sharee been trying to scare him on purpose?

He pulled his shoulders back, dabbed at his cheeks with the palm of one hand and tucked his phone closer to his ear. At some point he was going to have to think about what Sharee was trying to do to him, messing with his head like this, but not right now.

Not when the future of his baby was at stake.

"I don't understand what you're saying." His voice had dropped a good octave and he could barely force the words from his dry throat. "Cut to the chase."

"I'm not keeping her." Sharee huffed softly, as if even saying the words was an annoyance.

Her?

His baby was a girl?

His heart leaped into his throat, then danced in his chest with a melody all its own.

He was having a daughter!

Tears threatened to run free again, but he didn't even care. He hadn't cried since he was six years old and had flipped over on his bike. He'd skidded a good way on the asphalt. To a scared little boy, it looked as if everything was bleeding—his elbows, his knees, even his chin.

But his dad had grabbed him by the collar and shook

him, telling him that only girls cried and he'd better cowboy up.

Be a man.

And he had. No matter how badly he hurt, either inwardly or outwardly, he had never again shed a single tear.

Not until now, when the joy of knowing he had a daughter overflowed his spirit so strongly that it just had to find release somewhere.

His tears.

But—wait.

What?

The second part of what Sharee had said sideswiped him.

She wasn't going to keep their daughter?

He couldn't possibly have heard right. Had she really just said that?

He struggled to pull his thoughts back to earth in some semblance of order, but Sharee was already speaking again. Of course, she couldn't see what her words had done to him.

She had no clue.

"Seriously, Cash. What am I going to do with a baby? You might not know me all that well but trust me when I say I'm about the farthest thing from mother material there could possibly be, and I have *zero* interest in becoming one. I don't have a maternal bone in my body. As it is, this pregnancy is really messing up my life. I've gone from being perpetually nauseated to feeling like a clumsy elephant. I'm not even allowed to grab a beer with the boys. I hate every second of it."

Cash furrowed his brow. What Sharee was saying was a lot to take in, and none of it was good.

"You of all people should know my lifestyle isn't the least bit conducive for a baby. You know how much I like to follow the cowboys in pro rodeo from town to town. As if I would actually consider toting a baby around with me. Ha. I don't think so."

"Then what...?"

"I've already made up my mind to do a closed adoption. I'm going to give the baby away, and that's the end of it. I don't want a child trying to look me up eighteen years from now wanting to see what her real mama is like. No, thank you. Some nice family who wants a baby will take it home with them and that's the end of the subject."

Oh, no, it wasn't.

"You can't do that."

Panic shuddered through him. His stomach lurched, and bile burned in his throat. She'd called their daughter *the* baby. Not *her*, but *it*. She wasn't even affording their child the dignity of humanity.

"You can't tell me what to do," Sharee snapped, sounding irritated.

He had to grit his teeth to keep from telling her just *exactly* what she should do. He wanted to scream at her and let her know she had no right to take his baby away from him and he would never stand for it.

But yelling would only make things worse, so he forced himself to take a deep breath and slowly release it before he spoke. He needed to think logically.

Did she have the right to make the decision on her own?

What say did he have, as the baby's father? Surely, she couldn't give their daughter up for adoption without his consent.

Especially if he was ready to step up and take full custody of her.

In a momentary flash, his life had gone from trying to figure out how he was going to be a part of his baby's life to becoming the only parent who wanted his child.

Could he even *be* a single father?

Did he have it in him?

He wasn't even close to qualified. Cash hadn't had a great role model in his own father, who had been gone more than he'd been at home and wasn't devoted and loving to his family when he was.

But what other choice did he have?

There was no question that he would be there for his baby, whatever it took to fight for her custody. Cash's own flesh and blood would not go to an adoptive home when she had a biological father who already loved her.

He might not have the slightest idea what he was doing, but he *would* learn.

"Sharee," he said, his voice quivering despite his effort to remain calm and keep his tone neutral. "You never even gave me the courtesy of calling to ask me what I wanted to do regarding our child's custody."

He hoped his bitterness didn't creep through in his tone, because that would make his statement sound like an accusation, which, of course, it was.

"What difference does it make what you want?" she spat. "This isn't about you. Don't make it into something it isn't and complicate my life. The decision has been made. So drop it."

"I'm the baby's father."

This time there was no doubt that his frustration was roaring through his voice.

How could it not?

He clamped his jaw as tight as he could and squeezed his eyes shut, desperately trying to control the emotions hurtling through him.

"Is that what's got your goat?" She scoffed, and he could hear the derision dripping from her tone. "Then let me put you out of your misery. I'm not going to write your name on the birth certificate or on the adoption records. As far as every official document is concerned, you will not be listed as the baby's father. If someone asks, I'll say I don't know who the father is. The whole thing will all happen without you."

An ironic statement to make after she'd gone through all the trouble of announcing Cash as the baby's father on television and in magazines and ruined his career in the process.

"Sharee, I—"

The phone went dead in his hand. He dropped his cell to his lap and fisted his hands on the wheel, groaning in agony as he slumped over them, his forehead touching the backs of his hands and his knuckles burrowing into his eyes.

It was over for him.

All over.

He hadn't realized how important his baby was to him until just this moment.

When it was too late.

When he'd lost everything.

He wanted a drink so badly he was shaking. It occurred to him to call Frank, but what was he going to say? That his life was royally messed up and all he wanted to do was hide in some dark corner and nurse his wounds with a bottle of whiskey?

No. He was humiliated enough without admitting his faults to another person.

Somehow, some way, this was one fight he was going to have to win alone.

Emerson's was unusually slow, so Alyssa puttered around the shop, fronting shelves and restocking. With as small a town as Serendipity, the hardware store was a catchall for local residents, offering everything from large animal feed and farm tools to Western clothing and outerwear, including hats and boots. The Kickfire brand would be a huge new draw, which Alyssa hoped would solve the store's cash flow problems.

With such a variety of stock, keeping the store looking good took up the majority of Alyssa's time—any time that wasn't spent serving customers.

Which was just as well. At least she was never bored. And with Cash's help, they were keeping on top of the workload most of the time.

Thinking of Cash drew her mind into pondering what had been troubling him recently.

She knew beyond the shadow of a doubt that something was eating away at him. She'd always been unusually perceptive of the feelings of others, and she could sense Cash's agitation with every fiber of her being. It had been building for months, and she knew instinctively it was coming to a head.

She wished he would trust her enough to really let her in. How else would she be able to help and support him?

From what she'd seen the past few months Cash was putting all his effort into cleaning up his act. He might not realize it yet, but he was going to be a wonderful dad.

Fatherhood was a role he'd have to grow into, but wasn't that the case with all first-time parents? No one really knew what to expect out of parenthood until they held their own baby in their arms.

It was no different with Cash. As astonishing as it was, the formerly unreliable, selfish love-'em-and-leave-'em Cash Coble hadn't walked away from his responsibilities. Rather, he had not only acknowledged them, but was preparing for the ride of his life.

Fatherhood.

His biggest problem was that he didn't give himself enough credit because he no longer believed in himself. He didn't know this about himself, and if he did, he would never admit it, but he had the heart for it.

For love.

And that was all that really mattered. But there were many roadblocks ahead.

Alyssa was appalled by Sharee's hard-hearted cruelty in using her baby for her own gain.

Yet watching the way Cash's face had lit up when he spoke of his soon-to-be-born son or daughter was nothing short of wondrous, and Alyssa's heart had warmed like hot cocoa by the fireplace on a snowy winter's day.

He had not only taken full responsibility for his actions, but he recognized that despite everything, something good had come from it.

A new life.

A precious baby.

Cash was going to be a father, and that was a blessing from God.

Full stop.

She finished straightening a rack of ladies cowboy boots and glanced at her watch. Cash had been away for some time now, much longer than she'd anticipated. Over forty minutes had passed since he'd asked if he could take a break and had told her that he had a quick errand to run.

She had expected him back twenty minutes ago. Not that it was a huge issue for him to take a longer break if he wanted. Cash could use all the time he needed. She'd spent months running Emerson's by herself before Cash had come along at the auction, and a few more minutes of alone time wouldn't hurt her. In any case, not a single customer had come in while Cash was gone.

But when another fifteen minutes had passed, and Cash still hadn't returned, she started to get worried.

What kind of errand was so important that he'd had to rush out in the middle of a workday? And more to the point, why hadn't he come back to the store—or at least called to say he wouldn't be back in?

It was nearly quitting time anyway, so Alyssa turned the sign to Closed and quickly counted out the till and swept the floor, deciding she'd stop by the rented cabin on the Howells' land where Cash was staying and make sure he was all right.

To her surprise, when she exited the building and locked up, she turned to find Cash's pickup parked across the street and down a couple of spaces, just where it had been earlier in the morning.

He'd probably walked wherever he had planned to go. There weren't many places in Serendipity that a healthy person couldn't comfortably reach by foot, and Cash was definitely in good shape.

She covered a yawn with the back of her hand. Wherever Cash had gone, she could ask him about it in the morning. She was thoroughly exhausted, and she needed to check up on her father before heading back to her own apartment. She and Eddie had hired an in-home nurse to watch over Daddy, and Alyssa wanted to make sure he hadn't scared the poor woman off. He could be persnickety, especially if he felt like he was being ordered around.

In the best of all worlds, she would stop by the house and find her father complaining that he didn't need a nurse hovering over him. Maybe his fall and consequent recovery would help him snap out of the depression and grief that had been hanging over his head. He was making progress, but Alyssa couldn't help but want to rush it along.

She headed toward her own vehicle, anxious to get off her feet. A bowl of cold cereal and a brainless reality show on television sounded just about perfect right now.

As she turned to walk down the opposite side of the street from Cash's truck, a movement in the cab caught her eye.

At first, she thought it might only be the sunlight glinting off the windshield, but when she cupped her palm across her forehead to shade her eyes, she realized Cash was sitting behind the wheel.

She must have missed seeing him return. He'd probably noticed that she'd turned the sign to Closed and decided he'd come back to work in the morning.

Although Serendipity traffic was always light to nonexistent, she looked both ways before crossing to

Cash's truck, thinking she would let him know for certain that he wouldn't be needed until the following day.

When she was close enough to see Cash, her adrenaline spiked, and her heart leaped into her throat. She fished for her cell phone even as she rushed to the driver's side door and yanked at the handle.

It was locked.

Cash was slumped over the steering wheel, unmoving. A thousand different scenarios charged like a herd of wild horses through Alyssa's mind.

Was it a heart attack?

Unlikely. He was in the prime of his life and an athlete in excellent shape.

Had he somehow gotten into a fight and barely made it back to his truck?

Again, extremely unlikely. The crime rate in Serendipity was small, and a tussle that would leave Cash in this kind of condition was nearly unheard of.

Was it a brain aneurism?

Now she was scaring herself.

But what else could leave him passed out in his vehicle, unresponsive?

As she desperately pulled at the handle a second time, Cash stirred, slowly lifting his head and turning his unfocused gaze toward her. He stared right into her eyes but didn't appear to recognize her.

His eyes were red rimmed and bloodshot.

Had he been *drinking*?

Anger gripped her throat as any concern she'd been feeling for him rapidly faded. Her gaze swept the truck for any signs of alcohol. A bottle of whiskey or a six-pack of empty beer cans.

She didn't see any lingering evidence, but that didn't necessarily mean anything.

He'd *promised*.

And he'd been doing so well.

Then he'd walked off the job in the middle of the day and had not returned? That was almost a cliché.

Had he gone to a neighboring town and visited a bar or a liquor store?

How had she not suspected this? Or at least considered it as a possibility.

And just when she'd started to trust him.

How could he do this to her? She knew Cash's addiction wasn't about her, but she felt betrayed in the worst way. Her heart ached.

She pounded on the window and gestured for him to unlock the door.

He pressed his palms against his eyes, cringing as if he were staving off a raging headache, and then combed both hands back through his hair.

Finally, he reached for the handle and opened the door, but only a couple of inches.

Alyssa yanked it wide.

"Cash?"

He wavered, clenched one fist on the steering wheel and dropped his gaze to his lap, refusing to meet hers.

"Where have you been?" she demanded.

"I—" He shook his head. "Nowhere. Here." His voice was raw and gravelly.

"Are you trying to tell me you never left?"

"No, I—"

"Tell me the truth, Cash. Have you been drinking?"

"What? No. I—"

He sounded shocked that she would even ask, and

yet how could she believe him when she'd found him looking this way? Her eyes weren't lying to her.

"Have. You. Been. Drinking?" Speaking through gritted teeth, she made every word its own sentence.

Finally, he lifted his head and caught her gaze, holding it for a long time before he spoke.

"No."

"Then how do you explain—" She swished her hand back and forth, encompassing his entire frame, particularly his expression. "This."

He reached for her hand, but she jerked away from him. She knew if he touched her, sympathy for him would override her good sense. And right now, both of them needed her to be entirely rational.

"I want to drink," he admitted raggedly. "Every bone in my body is screaming for alcohol. I can't—I just can't deal right now."

"Deal with what?"

"I was just about ready to drive away when you walked up. Go to a neighboring town and visit a bar."

"You don't look like you're in any condition to drive," she said frankly, still not entirely convinced that he was telling her the truth.

"I've just been fooling myself," he said bitterly. "My career is trashed, and so is the rest of my life. I'll feel better after I've downed a whiskey or two."

"No. You won't." She wasn't sure whether she was telling him he wouldn't feel better after having a couple of drinks, or whether she was assuring him he wouldn't be visiting a bar anytime soon.

Not if she could help it.

Maybe it was both.

"Just leave me alone."

"Like this?" She shook her head emphatically. "I don't think so. Unlock the passenger door. I'm coming in."

She rounded the front of his truck to keep him from gunning the engine and driving away without her and slid onto the seat beside him, tucking one leg beneath her and turning to face him.

"Did you call your sponsor?" The only facts Alyssa knew about an alcoholic's twelve-step program were what she'd seen on television, but it was enough to know all alcoholics had someone they could call, any time of the day or night, if they found themselves fighting the urge to drink, as Cash clearly was.

"I don't have one. I don't do Alcoholics Anonymous."

"Why not?"

He snorted. "Are you kidding me? If I went to an AA meeting, word would get out and my already tattered career would be obliterated. Martin is trying to keep this on the down low. And that means I'm dealing with this myself—which is what I would do, anyway. Group meetings aren't my thing."

"Has Martin seen you in the state you are in right now?"

Cash shook his head. "No. And he wouldn't care if he did. Not about me, anyway. The only thing that matters to him is my image and getting me back under rodeo sponsorship so he can take his cut of the money I make."

That didn't ring true to Alyssa. Surely the relationship between an agent and a cowboy ought to be one of mutual respect, at least. Although after seeing Martin with Cash, she supposed she shouldn't be surprised.

The next time she saw Martin she was going to

have a word with him—probably many words. Martin ought to count his blessings that she wasn't the type of woman who would physically throttle him, because the urge to do so surged through her veins.

She'd had no idea just how hard Cash had been wrestling with his addiction to alcohol. It ran much deeper than she could ever have imagined.

And to expect him to face that battle alone? That was cruel and unusual punishment.

Clearly, Cash needed help, whether he was willing to admit it or not. Forget what Martin thought, or even Cash, in his willful stubbornness, believing he could face this all on his own.

He couldn't. Whether he was ready to admit it or not, he needed other people.

She would gladly step up to support Cash, but even if she made a special effort to learn about alcoholism—which she intended to do—Alyssa wasn't sure she would be able to be the right person to give him the kind of support he needed.

"I don't think your image is what you should be concerned about right now," Alyssa stated frankly.

"What about spending some time in a rehab center?" she asked. "That seems to be a big thing with the actors in Hollywood, and their careers don't appear to be affected by it. If anything, it's publicity. All publicity is good publicity, right?"

He snorted. "Not for me, it isn't." He locked his gaze with hers. "No rehab facility for me. That's not how I'm going to do this thing."

"O-kay." She drew the word out in frustration. Why wouldn't the man admit when he needed help, as he so clearly did now? Couldn't he see that he couldn't walk alone?

"But," he continued, reaching out a hand and stroking the back of one finger across her jaw, "I am glad you found me when you did. Otherwise, I might have— *would* have—gone to the nearest town and spent the evening on a bar stool in front of a tumbler of whiskey."

"Which is exactly why you can't do this yourself. You need to surround yourself with people who care for you."

Panic flashed across his expression, but he quickly schooled his features.

He might think he could do it alone, but Alyssa was just as positive he could not. And Martin was not the person to speak to about her concerns.

Maybe Jo Spencer would have a good idea. Alyssa certainly had no clue, nor had she ever felt so helpless.

"Do you want to tell me what happened?" she asked, feeling as if she was getting nowhere.

She still wondered about his bloodshot eyes. If he hadn't been drinking, then what…?

"I called Sharee again," he admitted. "After you and I had our conversation, I felt I needed to take the initiative to reach out to her and make sure I connected this time. In the past, I've let it slide when my call has gone to voice mail, but now I see what a bad idea that was. The last thing I should have done was to give her enough space to make all the decisions about *our* baby on her own."

He blew out a frustrated breath. "I did finally get a hold of her. I called over and over until she answered. And then I found out—" His voice cracked. "The situation is worse, even than I could have possibly imagined."

"How is that?"

His beautiful azure eyes pooled with moisture.

That explained his red-rimmed eyes.

He hadn't been drinking.

He'd been *crying*.

She didn't think less of him for it. It took a strong man to process his emotions, especially since he no longer had his usual backup—alcohol.

She didn't know what to do to help him.

Oh, Lord. Be with Cash right now. Comfort him and give him Your peace.

"Sharee has already made arrangements for our daughter to be given away in a closed adoption."

"It's a girl?" she asked, her voice catching.

Despite everything, he smiled shakily.

"Yeah. I have a baby girl on the way. Can you believe it?" Moisture appeared on his forehead and his chest heaved. He was hyperventilating.

"Breathe, Cash. No matter what Sharee told you, she can't just give your baby up for adoption without your consent. It will only take a simple swab test to confirm paternity. You are the baby's biological father. You have rights."

Alyssa knew zilch about adoption laws, but she was certain the biological father would have a say in what happened to his daughter. Surely Cash must have the right to claim the custody of his child if that was what he wanted.

"Not according to Sharee. She said she's not putting my name down as father on either the birth certificate or the adoption papers, and she'll deny my baby's paternity if she's pressed on the issue."

That woman should be ashamed of herself.

"Are you kidding me? After she spread it all over the news that you got her pregnant? That is the stupidest thing I've ever heard."

"Yeah. I thought the same thing."

"Okay," Alyssa said, inhaling a calming breath and letting it out slowly. "There's no way she's going to get away with this. It doesn't matter what she does or does not write on the birth certificate when we can easily get biological proof. We just need to figure out what to do next."

His gaze widened, and he brushed the tears from his cheeks with his shirtsleeve.

"We?" His glossy eyes brightened, and his Adam's apple bobbed as he swallowed convulsively.

"Of course." She reached for his hand and squeezed it. "I'm here for you, Cash. Whatever you need—starting with meeting Sharee face-to-face. We're going to fight this. You're going to win full custody of your daughter."

She wished she felt as confident as she sounded. In truth, she had no idea what the future held.

Thankfully, she knew Who did.

Chapter Eight

Cash surveyed himself in the mirror, brushing a piece of imaginary lint off the shoulder of the best burgundy-colored chambray shirt he owned. He narrowed his eyes on his reflection, thoughtfully appraising himself before straightening his cowboy hat, which he'd brushed clean the night before.

His gut churned, and he swallowed back the burn in his throat.

He didn't know why he was putting this much effort into his appearance. In general, he rarely gave a thought to what he wore or how he looked. And it wasn't as if he was going before a judge or anything.

Not yet, anyway.

Why was today different? What did it matter how he was dressed? Yet some unnamed emotion urged him to do whatever he could to look his best.

Part of it, he privately admitted, *might* have to do with Alyssa. She'd be the first one to see him today. Her natural, unassuming beauty had caught his eye more times than he could count. What would it feel like if she noticed him as more than the man she had won in an auction, a man who had been nothing but trouble for her?

But that was dangerous thinking, and there was no way he would go there.

He couldn't.

Alyssa was an incredibly thoughtful, sensitive woman and deserved the very best in life, including an honorable, straight-as-an-arrow Christian husband with whom to build a stable, loving family.

Everything he was not, in other words.

Alyssa had a quiet strength about her—another attractive quality, and one of many. He still couldn't believe she was willing to stand by him during one of the biggest crises of his life.

One of them.

Despite his best efforts to the contrary, his thoughts flashed to Aaron, and the whole reason he'd been involved with Sharee in the first place. He would never have imagined that what started out as two friends fighting over a girl they didn't even know would have such long-lasting consequences.

Unwanted memories washed over him as he recalled every detail of that fateful night when Aaron had gotten behind the wheel of his car and had driven off after having far too much to drink. How he had missed a stop sign and had crashed headlong into a semi. The single blessing, if one could call it that, was that the doctors had said Aaron had died instantly, with no suffering.

But all those memories brought Cash right back to the present and his relationship with Alyssa. He needed to tread very carefully where his friendship with her was concerned.

Aaron's death was the main reason he had to nip his attraction to Alyssa in the bud, even more than Cash knowing she deserved better than him.

He couldn't be with her.

Not now.

Not ever.

If he was dressing to look his best today, it was to demonstrate to Sharee, however subconsciously, that he had his act together.

That he was responsible and had what it took to be a good father to their daughter.

Even if in truth, he didn't.

When he'd first discovered he was going to be a daddy, he'd thought he would have more time to try to learn all the ins and outs of caring for an infant, to read all of the bestselling baby books and maybe spend time with some of his friends' babies.

But not now. There wasn't a minute to waste. He could no longer wait until he felt ready.

This situation had to be resolved now.

Today.

Whether he was ready or not.

He heard Alyssa honking her horn from out in front of his cabin and his shoulders slumped in relief. He was so grateful she had offered to be here with him today. He inhaled deeply, then let the air out slowly.

With Alyssa standing beside him, he could do this.

She had offered to drive, which he'd happily taken her up on. He was so shaky he wasn't certain he could have handled the wheel if he'd tried, never mind the accelerator. That was all he needed, to mindlessly drive into a ditch because his thoughts were elsewhere.

He had called Sharee back and they'd arranged to meet.

Cash and Alyssa were making the trip to Dallas, where Sharee was currently living, with the intention of convincing her he really did want full custody of his daughter. Hopefully if she saw him in person, she would realize how much he'd changed.

Getting to the weekend seemed to take forever. He'd had far too much alone time during the past couple of days—every second he wasn't at Emerson's working with Alyssa—to mull over what would happen.

He couldn't eat. He couldn't sleep.

He had imagined every possible scenario, every way this confrontation could go wrong.

He was worried about distressing the baby when they met with Sharee, knowing Sharee would get all worked up about them being there. He hated the idea that his presence might have a negative effect on the child, but he couldn't see any way around that.

It had to be done. There was no other way he could see to make things right.

He hoped she wouldn't panic and accelerate her plans to sign the adoption papers before they had the opportunity to talk things through.

Could she do that?

He had no idea when those legal proceedings happened.

Before the baby's birth, or afterward?

He prayed he wouldn't ever have to know. If necessary, he would be contacting a family lawyer to discuss his options once he knew where Sharee's head was at.

"You look terrible," Alyssa remarked as he slid into the passenger seat of the cab.

Despite his anxiety, his mouth jerked into a wry half smile.

"Well, thank you for that. And here I spent extra time primping in front of the mirror this morning."

The pathetic part of that statement was that it was true.

Her cheeks colored an attractive shade of rose.

"That's not what I meant," she chided softly. "You're handsome and you know it. I don't think anyone needs to boost your ego in that department."

Not *anyone*. But he did like hearing it from *Alyssa*.

"You clean up very nicely—although I'm wondering if you ought to roll down the window and hang your head out to get some fresh air. You're green around the gills."

That didn't sound like a half-bad idea.

He groaned and clutched at his stomach. "I feel like I'm going to be sick. This is worse than any hangover I've ever experienced."

"It's nerves. You'll be okay." She put the truck into gear and headed for the highway.

She sounded so convinced of what she was saying. He only wished he felt the same assurance.

"I wish I believed that. I stand to lose my very own flesh and blood today and I have absolutely no control about how this is going to go down."

She glanced over at him and then back at the road. "You might not know what the future holds, but I know Someone who does."

"Who?"

"I'm talking about God. I'm not going to get up on a soapbox and tell you what you should believe. I can only show you what He has done for me. Right now, He's giving me peace. Otherwise, I'd be totally tripping out and wouldn't be able to breathe, much less drive."

"You really think God's got this?"

She nodded vigorously. "Oh, I know He does. I'm not saying everything that happens today will be perfect and we won't have any conflict with Sharee. We very well may run into trouble. It's hard to say, given everything I've heard about that woman. But I do know God wants that sweet, soon-to-be-born baby girl to stay with her biological father—a daddy who loves her."

She flicked a glance at him. "And I want you to know I'm going to fight with every last ounce of my being to make sure that happens."

"I wish—" He paused and sighed softly. "I wish—"

He didn't know how to put what he wanted to say into words, to explain how he was feeling right now, so in the end, he clenched one arm around his middle, stared out the passenger window and let his words drop into silence.

Alyssa reached across the cab and squeezed his hand. He didn't know if it was only meant to be a quick, comforting gesture, but he laced his fingers through hers. He needed human contact right now.

"We've got a big project to do next week," Alyssa said conversationally. "It's time to dig through my shed and get out all the Christmas decorations for the store."

"All of them?" He groaned. "What are we talking about? A box of tinsel and garland and a string of lights?"

He appreciated that she was trying to distract him but talking about Christmas wasn't the way to do it. He'd never cared for the season because he'd never really seen the point. His parents had never done much for him when he was a kid. They went to the midnight Christmas church service and that was about it. Mama had a soft heart toward God, but his dad ran a tight household, and he'd never had much use for religion. So his mom had done what she could, but it wasn't much.

As an adult, they did even less together. They didn't even get together for the holidays, which meant Cash would spend his Christmas alone.

Ho, ho, *horrible*.

"Among other things. What's wrong? You don't like Christmas, Cowboy McScrooge?"

His lips twitched into a smile. "Something like that."

"Then I'll make it my personal mission to convert you into a Christmas-loving cowboy. I always bring in a live evergreen to the store and decorate it to the hilt. You name it—ornaments, lights, garland, tinsel. I string hundreds of blinking lights all around the inside and outside of the shop and place a large nativity scene in the front window. Of course, this year we'll also have our Kickfire display."

"That's right. The big debut is coming up, isn't it? Black Friday?"

"Yes, and I can hardly wait."

"Yeah. Me, either."

"Buzzkill. You don't exactly sound enthused."

"Oh, I will be, or at least I'll look like I am, all dressed up in my Kickfire gear. I haven't forgotten that I'm serving as your face for the grand opening. Pete will be there with his camera and a film crew from the local news, too."

"Really?" Her face brightened, and Cash was glad he'd gone to the extra effort of bringing in a news crew. This wasn't just about a promise anymore.

"Thank you," she whispered.

"For what?"

"For everything."

"I should be thanking you." He squeezed her hand.

They rode in silence for the rest of the trip, each lost in their own thoughts. Cash mentally rehearsed everything he intended to say to Sharee once they were speaking face-to-face. Trying to remember every line of reasoning he would propose. What he would say when she raised her objections, as he knew she would. Just thinking about it was making every muscle in his body bind up in painful knots.

"Here we are," she said, pulling into a vacant parking spot in the middle of a beat-up apartment complex in what was clearly a not-so-great neighborhood in a bad part of town. The place didn't look very well kept up, with faded yellow siding peeling away from the wall, and dirt and dandelions poking up where the landscaping ought to be.

Cash didn't move, except to reach for the truck handle. He gritted his teeth and managed to tighten his grip but didn't open the door.

Alyssa cleared her throat. "I know I can't even begin to imagine how difficult this must be for you, so I'm not going to say otherwise. All I can tell you is to embrace what is happening and seek God through it all. Believe that the Lord has His best planned for you and for your precious baby. This may be the day you look back on as the day you claimed paternity of your little baby. The first day of the rest of your lives together as a family."

Or, conversely, this might be the worst day of his entire life.

Their gazes met and held, and he could tell she was

thinking the same thing, even if she wasn't willing to voice her thoughts.

This could be the day he lost everything.

Alyssa's stress level was off the charts. She wasn't even certain she and Cash had made the right decision coming here. There were far more ways this scenario could go wrong than having it go right, and she thought she'd probably considered every last one of them.

But what else could Cash do?

He was that baby's biological father and he wanted his daughter. He was going to have to fight for her.

Alyssa didn't share her fears with Cash. She could see by his expression he was having the same thoughts as she was, and he was the one with everything to lose. She wished she could do more for him than just support him and stand by his side.

When Cash didn't immediately exit the cab after they'd pulled up in front of Sharee's apartment, Alyssa used the moment to center herself in prayer. She had to be strong for Cash—not in her own strength but with Christ's strength within her and through her.

"Are you ready?" she queried softly.

He blew out a breath. "No. Not even close. I need a drink, and I'm not sure how I'm going to get through this without one."

She tilted her head, regarding him closely. "You really think that would help?"

His gaze met hers. "No. Not really. But I've used alcohol as my coping mechanism for so many months that it's hard not to be tempted."

"Of course you're tempted. Not giving in to that feeling is the hard part."

"Right."

"I know you have to mentally prepare yourself for what may lie ahead. I'm not in a hurry. You can take as long as you need."

"That's half the problem," he admitted. "I *have* been mentally preparing myself—which inevitably leads to my thinking of all the ways this could go wrong."

Alyssa definitely empathized and wondered if she should reveal those emotions.

No. He already knew she was here to support him. She didn't think it would be helpful to speak about things they had no control over.

He jerked his chin in a firm nod.

"Let's do this."

He and Alyssa exited the truck and searched for the numbers on the apartment doors until they found Sharee's.

Cash hesitated once again when they reached the landing in front of her apartment and Alyssa tucked her hand beneath his elbow. An old, dusty gray mat with cowboy boots and horseshoes offered a welcome Alyssa did not feel.

"Here goes nothing," Cash muttered under his breath before clenching his jaw and knocking four times in rapid succession.

Behind the door, Alyssa heard the shuffle of feet. The door didn't have a peephole, nor was there a window in front, so Sharee wouldn't have the opportunity to see who was knocking without opening the door.

"It's about time," Sharee said as she flung open the door. "I'm starving. What is it with you people that it takes you an hour to deliver one pizza? Did you have to harvest the grain to make the crust?"

"Hello, Sharee," Cash said, his voice low and gruff with emotion. "I'm afraid your pizza will have to wait. Did you forget we agreed to meet today?"

"Oh. Right. Come in, then."

Alyssa didn't know what she'd expected Sharee to look like, but this was not it. It was one o'clock in the afternoon and Sharee was still in pink cotton pajamas, her hair was rumpled and her makeup was smeared. Her pajamas didn't appear to be of the maternity variety, and Sharee's round belly pressed against the buttons.

When Sharee stepped away from the door, Cash didn't hesitate in marching straight into the apartment, looking back only once to make sure Alyssa was following.

Which she was—close enough to reach out and grab the back of his shirt. If he stopped suddenly she would run straight into him. Her nerves were starting to get to her.

Sharee didn't look like the type of woman with whom a person could hold a rational conversation. Not today, in any case.

"Where would you like to talk?" Cash asked, keeping his voice neutral. If he was feeling the same anxiety, he was no longer showing it.

Sharee gestured toward a blue sofa that had definitely seen better days, its fabric worn at the corners and ripped in some places.

Cash sat first, and then Alyssa sank into the seat next to him.

Not a bad idea, showing Sharee a united front. And if the pregnant woman got any other ideas from Cash's gesture, well, Alyssa wouldn't lie about it, but she saw no reason to blurt out the truth—that she and Cash were just friends—good friends. Having a woman at Cash's side couldn't hurt their argument for him gaining custody of his child.

Sharee supported the underside of her stomach as she awkwardly settled in an armchair across from them. With a groan, she combed her hair back with her thumb and index finger, then leaned her elbow on the arm of the chair and rested her chin in her hand.

"I have to say, I agreed to see you, Cash, but in all honesty, I'm not sure why you're here." Sharee's ice-blue eyes bored into Cash's.

Alyssa had assumed Cash would take the lead in this conversation and was a little thrown off that Sharee had spoken first.

Cash cleared his throat and met Sharee's gaze squarely. "Before we go any further, I need to apologize to you for my actions. I'm sorry for the way I treated you when we first met. Everything that happened that night—" He paused as his voice cracked. "I recognize that I'm responsible for my part in it."

Sharee scoffed.

"But since that time, I've done everything in my power to make up for what I did, to become a better man. And that includes wanting to take full custody of our daughter."

"Full custody?" Sharee exclaimed. "You're kidding, right?"

"He's serious," Alyssa said.

"Excuse me? Who are you?" Sharee speared Alyssa with her gaze. How had Cash gotten tangled up with a woman like her?

"She's—" Cash started, and then faltered.

"I'm Alyssa Emerson, a friend of Cash's," she finished for him. "We work together."

Confusion crossed Sharee's expression, and then what looked to Alyssa like a touch of jealousy. Her eyes settled on Cash's arm, which was still around Alyssa's shoulders.

"Where is this, exactly? At the rodeo? I didn't know Cash was back on tour. I thought he was doing some charity work to shine up his tarnished image."

"Can't keep anything a secret," Cash muttered under his breath. And then, louder, "Yes, that is the plan. I'm working at Alyssa's store as part of my publicity campaign."

He made it sound like that was all that it was. Alyssa's shoulders tightened, and Cash glanced down at her, concern etched in his face. Now was not the time to react to being summarily placed back on the advertising burner. Alyssa had thought they'd gone far past that, that they really *were* good friends.

Apparently not.

"And then you're planning to return to the rodeo." Sharee's words weren't a question.

"That's the plan. I'm putting my past behind me, and I still have a few good years left to succeed at bareback bronc riding. If I win, I can make enough money to seed our daughter's college fund."

It was as if a fist squeezed Alyssa's heart. She'd known from the moment Cash had stepped into her life that he was there to repair his image. The end game was his return to the rodeo circuit.

When had her thoughts—and her heart—changed?

It was only just recently that Alyssa had started seriously considering another outcome—one of Cash staying in Serendipity with his daughter, making the town his home and the store his permanent employment. As far as Alyssa was concerned, there wasn't a better place on Earth to raise a family.

They hadn't discussed it yet, but the rodeo circuit was no place for a newborn baby. Had Cash even considered what he would do with his daughter when he was out on the circuit? Was that what Sharee had been thinking about when she'd decided on adoption?

Maybe the woman wasn't as far out there as Alyssa had first assumed. Still, Cash seemed determined to raise his own child, even if he hadn't offered all the specifics.

Alyssa looked from one to the other of them. They appeared to be in some sort of mental standoff, their gazes locked and yet not a single word spoken between them.

"Then I'm doing you a favor," Sharee said at last. "Think about it, Cash. You can't take a baby with you on the rodeo circuit. It would only get in your way."

"My daughter is not an inconvenience," Cash whispered, his voice cracking with strain. "And I'm not willing to walk away from my responsibility to her."

"That's why I'm giving you an out. You don't *have* a responsibility to her. She will be going to a good home and you can get on with your life, live it up like you used to. No worries."

"That will never happen," he assured her. His voice was so quiet and so controlled that Alyssa shivered. "I'm not the man I used to be. I'm going to be a father to our daughter."

His arm tightened around Alyssa's shoulders.

"And I'm keeping my baby," Cash said.

Chapter Nine

Cash had never been so frustrated in his whole life, and his mind and body were screaming for a drink.

He'd known this confrontation would be difficult, but he'd had no idea Sharee would be so completely unmoved. No matter how rationally he tried to discuss the subject, Sharee just brushed him off.

Not only him, but their baby.

Unbelievable.

She was right about one thing. It would be next to impossible for him to take his daughter on the rodeo circuit. His baby needed the stability of a home and a father who would always be there for her. He couldn't provide that for her if he was gone all the time, and he wasn't going to let her be raised by a nanny.

But he couldn't stand the thought of him not being in his daughter's life, of someone else raising his child. If there were changes to be made to make custody possible, they were his to make.

As hard as it might be for him personally, he would sacrifice his career for his daughter in a heartbeat. He didn't know what that would look like in reality. The only thing he'd ever known was rodeo.

He now realized he should have thought the matter through before his meeting with Sharee. He should have been able to tell her exactly how he planned on raising their daughter, to show Sharee how much he'd changed.

He wanted to prove he could be a stable and loving father to their baby, because all that Sharee had ever known of him was a pompous, bigheaded cowboy who thought of no one but himself. A partyer and a playboy.

He was ashamed just to think about it.

He took his arm off from around Alyssa's shoulder and clenched his fists between his knees, desperately combating his emotions. Seeing Sharee's baby bump and knowing his daughter was about to be born choked him up, even without facing down the fear that he might never get to see his baby grow up.

"I understand you want to give your and Cash's daughter up in a closed adoption." Alyssa took over the conversation, speaking in a hushed but rational tone.

"That's right. I want to put all this behind me." Sharee gestured to her stomach.

"I know you do," Alyssa said softly. "And that's all well and good. But we've come here today to offer you another solution."

"Cash and I have already discussed this on the phone," Sharee snapped.

No. No, they had not.

Sharee had done all the talking the other day. Cash had been too devastated by what he'd been told to hold anywhere close to a real conversation. And he certainly hadn't agreed with her conclusions.

"Yes. And you want a closed adoption, so the child will have no way to connect with you when they are old enough to do so."

Sharee smiled for the first time that day. "Exactly. I'm glad you understand."

Cash didn't get it. Not at all. How could Sharee not want to be part of her baby's life?

"That's just the thing," Alyssa said, her voice calm. She brushed her palms across the fabric of her jeans. "I don't understand. And I'm not sure you've thought this all the way through, either."

"Oh, believe me, I have."

Cash wanted to say something but his mouth wouldn't form words. He felt as if he was ready to jump out of his skin.

"I believe you," Alyssa said gently. "We understand why at present, a baby would feel like a burden to you. But there is another option—a *better* one—than choosing a closed adoption."

"I'm not doing an open adoption, so you can just forget that," Sharee snapped.

It was hard enough for Cash to imagine his daughter growing up without a mother. But at least she would have a father who loved her and would show her how much he loved her every day of her life.

"I'm going to assert my rights as the biological father of our daughter," he blurted out roughly, wishing he had half the self-control Alyssa was displaying.

"Why would you do that?" Sharee looked and sounded legitimately stunned. "You're in the same position as I am. You can't possibly want to raise a kid right now."

"But I do" Cash said. "God blessed us with a baby,

and I'm not letting my daughter go to another home, even if it's a good one. She *has* a home. With me."

"This really is the best-case scenario all around," Alyssa added. "We understand—er, Cash does, I mean—what an inconvenience this baby would be to you now. And he expects nothing from you. If you don't want him to tell her about you, he won't. Not ever."

"But if you ever did want me to tell her a little bit about you, anything I tell our daughter about her mother will be positive. That, I can promise you."

"I don't want her to know anything about me," Sharee insisted.

"The decision will always be yours," Cash assured her. "I won't ever break my promise to you to keep your identity a secret."

"I'd rather not have to make this a huge battle between us," Cash said, keeping his voice low and even. "I have the right to the custody of my daughter whether you respect that fact or not. I don't want to have to do it, but I will block any attempt at adoption and will be ready to do a paternity test the moment our baby is born. Either way, it's going to happen. Fighting me over it is a waste of your time, and mine."

"I'm going to have to think about this," Sharee said, rubbing a hand absently over her belly. "I want you to realize I really am thinking of our baby, here," Sharee said, the acerbic tone leaving her voice. "I believed, and still believe, that she should go to a good home, with two parents who really want a baby and who will love her and take care of her."

"*I* will love her and take care of her."

"I don't know, Cash. I'm just not seeing it. You'll be a single father. And more to the point, how can an egotistical drunk who gets in a fight with his best friend over a girl suddenly turn into a man responsible enough to be a father to a newborn? That's not something that can happen overnight."

Her words sent Cash reeling. She had just touched on his biggest fear—that he wasn't good enough.

And to top it off, she'd gutted him with his guilt over Aaron's death. A secret Alyssa didn't yet know about.

"He'll have help," Alyssa told Sharee. "We live in a small town where friends and neighbors are like family. And, of course, he'll have the full support of our local church."

Alyssa smiled reassuringly and reached for his hand. "And he has me, for what that's worth."

A burst of emotion surged through him like a bolt of electricity. Alyssa had no idea what her support was worth to him. He had no words to express his feelings to her, what she meant to him.

"I think you should leave now. I'll get back to you," Sharee said.

"What does that mean?" Cash asked.

"You've really thrown a wrench into my plans. I don't know which way is up or down right now. You say you've got the right to obtain full custody, but is that really true, given your recent history? What would a judge say about all this? I just don't know yet. You have to give me some time to figure this out."

"Not too much time," he warned, his heart beating frantically. "I can and will fight for my paternity."

"Yes, but if I'm not mistaken, I could go to court and present evidence demonstrating that you shouldn't have custody, and it would be better for our daughter to be adopted."

Could she really prove him unworthy of custody? And the more frightening question—*would* she? She was one of the very few who knew what had really happened that night with Aaron.

Sharee knew his secret. If word got out...

No. He couldn't change the past, and he wouldn't give up the fight for his daughter. She was his future.

He'd given Sharee good reasons not to fight him on this. He could only hope she'd see the wisdom in his words, and that she would feel it was too much of a hassle to take legal action against him.

He prayed this wouldn't turn out to be an all-out battle, because it was one he might lose.

Alyssa was proud of Cash for the way he'd handled himself with Sharee. There was a time in the not so distant past where he wouldn't have had the self-control to not lose his temper or make harsh demands.

Things had not gone quite as on-script as she had hoped for, but it seemed to her that Sharee now realized Cash was serious about wanting custody of his daughter and it was only a matter of time before she gave in.

It still galled Alyssa that Sharee thought of an innocent infant as an inconvenience. But it was that fact that might work the most in Cash's favor. Sharee had threatened to take him to court, but why would she go to that much effort when Cash was stepping up to virtually take away her troubles?

Alyssa expected Cash to look at least a little bit relieved by the progress they'd made today, though of course everything had been left up in the air. But instead of appearing less stressed than earlier in the day, he was staring out the passenger window with a grim expression on his face.

"She's going to capitulate, you know."

He merely grunted in response.

She tried again.

"Today was a win. You have to see that."

He didn't even give her a verbal response this time.

"We should go out and celebrate, maybe catch dinner at Cup O' Jo's."

That got his attention, anyway. He turned toward her, his gaze incredulous.

"You think we ought to be happy about the way things went down today?"

"Of course I do. It won't take her long to realize you taking custody is the best option for your baby, if she doesn't recognize that already. At the very least, I believe she'll relent because it's too much of an inconvenience and an expense to fight you. But maybe she'll come to realize that it's the best thing for everyone, even for her."

Cash scoffed. "I highly doubt that."

"I think her threat of taking you to court is all hot air. It would be too much of a hassle for her, not to mention that you can prove you're a competent father. So even if it went that far, you'll still get custody of your daughter."

"I'm not so sure about that."

"Well, at any rate," she said, "I'm starving, and I need to eat. Are you going to join me or not?"

He paused before answering, his gaze becoming distant again.

"I guess so." She'd never heard him sound quite so

apathetic, even during the first days she'd worked with him at the store.

"Don't let me twist your arm or anything."

"What?" He looked at her as if she were speaking Greek.

Alyssa shook her head. "Nothing. Don't worry about it."

Wow. Sharee really had done a number on him. Cash never talked to her about his relationship with Sharee, but now Alyssa wondered if his feelings for the mother of his child ran deeper than she'd assumed.

Alyssa wasn't prepared for the tide of emotions that washed over her at the thought of Cash having feelings for another woman. She had no claim on Cash and had never really considered the way her feelings for him had grown, and yet…

She'd really come to depend on him over the past months. They'd developed a close friendship and had deep conversations along with their laughter and teasing. She liked having him around and spending time with him.

But what she was feeling now couldn't be labeled as merely friendship.

She really *cared* for him. And even though her emotions were only now catching up with her, she had wondered a time or two whether a man like Cash could ever be interested in her.

Cash was a man who'd always caught the eye of the public, especially the ladies. He was a handsome, outgoing soul who could make anyone smile, with very little effort on his part—even if, when he'd first started working with her, he hadn't always been in a good mood.

But could he grow to feel something special for her?

After seeing Sharee, the answer was *clearly not*.

"I'm sorry," Cash apologized, his voice husky.

Alyssa was jolted back to the present and her heart hammered, wondering if Cash had seen the way her thoughts had drifted off. Hopefully he hadn't read anything embarrassing in her expression.

That was all she needed, for Cash to catch her mooning over him.

"Why are you apologizing?" she asked, confused. She wondered if she'd missed something between her invitation to dinner and his answer.

"It's not you. It's been a long day, and I'm not very hungry. But there's something we need to—that is— would you like to take a walk with me?"

Alyssa immediately agreed. Whatever was burdening Cash, maybe talking it out would do him some good.

She pulled up and parked in front of the store, behind Cash's truck.

"Where would you like to go?" she asked. "The park has a nice greenbelt and bike path that joggers seem to like. Not that I would know. If I run, you'll know it's because a wild beast is chasing me."

If she'd hoped to get a chuckle out of him, she failed miserably.

"The park will be fine."

He tucked both hands into the front pockets of his jeans and stepped off the curb, jaywalking across the street. To her surprise, he didn't even check the road for traffic, much less look back to see if she was following.

She walked over to the three-way light—the only one in Serendipity—and crossed on the crosswalk. It was a silly thing, she supposed, but she'd always been the type to follow the letter of the law.

Thankfully, Cash wasn't walking very fast. If he'd been treading at his normal pace she never would have caught up with him after waiting for the light to turn. As it was, she only had to lengthen her stride to reach his side.

He appeared rigid and closed off, his shoulders stiff and his jaw set, and Alyssa wasn't sure how to reach him.

Tentatively, she linked her arm with his. He didn't acknowledge it, or her, but then again, he didn't pull away. He just kept walking until they'd reached the relative privacy of a grove of trees along either side of the bike path.

"Do you want to tell me what's bothering you?" she asked gently.

He sighed deeply and turned to her, taking both of her hands in his.

"There's something I need to tell you." His gaze darkened to a midnight blue as the corners of his lips turned down.

Alyssa's muscles instinctively tightened. His tone suggested that whatever he had to say was something she would not want to hear.

The long pause confirmed it.

"Okay. I'm listening."

He winced, and his fingers trembled in hers.

"I really want a drink right now."

That wasn't what she expected him to say, but maybe it should have been. At least he acknowledged it.

"You don't need one," she assured him. "There's nothing you can tell me that will change the way I feel about you."

She swallowed hard. Though she was completely

sincere in her assertion, she wasn't sure that was the right thing to say. She shouldn't be admitting that she had feelings for him if he was about to admit he was struggling over how he felt about Sharee.

She prepared herself for the worst, shielding her heart as best she could, and tried again.

"What I mean is, you can tell me anything," she clarified. "And I promise I won't judge."

Cash had been judged enough in his life.

Hadn't she been exactly that person the first few days after he'd returned to Serendipity? He needed someone who would be there for him through thick and thin, who would listen to him even if she didn't always have the answers.

If Alyssa could be that person, she would.

He groaned and shifted his gaze to somewhere over her left shoulder. "You're going to hate me."

"Never."

Alyssa couldn't imagine what he was talking about. Nothing he could ever do would make her hate him.

Had he fallen off the wagon and she didn't know about it? Or was it because he'd seen Sharee today and he was still in love with her?

"Well, thank you for that," he muttered under his breath.

"Does this have to do with Sharee?" she probed tenderly. "Are you still in love with her?"

"What? No!" he exclaimed so fast, and with such fervor, that there was no doubt in Alyssa's mind that he felt nothing for Sharee. His eyes were on hers again and she could clearly see how shocked he was that she'd even asked the question.

"Okay. I believe you."

Alyssa was relieved that she had misinterpreted Cash's mood and the uninterrupted silence on the long drive back to Serendipity.

"To be honest, I've never really known what it's like to love someone. To care for them enough to put them above my own needs. It's always been about me. But now, finding out about my baby…" He coughed. "And then these past few months spending time with you—"

He paused, and his eyes lightened to a twilight color, in between azure and midnight blue. With infinite gentleness, he ran one hand up her arm and over her shoulder. His fingers curved around the back of her neck, and he used his thumb to tilt her chin up to better meet his gaze.

"This," he said, using his other hand to draw her palm to his chest and press it on the spot just over his heart, "has been dead for so long that I barely recognized it when it sparked back to life."

"I don't—" she started, but he shook his head.

"I am not in a place where I can make any kind of promises to you. I'm not a man you should, or even could, look to for anything resembling a relationship."

"But—"

Again, he interrupted her, but this time it wasn't with words. He bent his forehead to touch hers and gazed into her eyes.

Slowly, softly, gently, he brushed his lips over hers.

She'd been waiting for this moment for a long time, probably even before she'd realized that this was what she wanted.

She sighed softly and leaned into his caress, allowing him to draw her fully into his arms as she wrapped herself around his waist and hugged him tight.

How had she missed the feelings growing between them, when it was so clear now that he felt the same way she did?

Emotions like these didn't suddenly appear out of nowhere. Up until this moment, she hadn't considered starting a romantic relationship with him, something that might even hold the promise of a future. But now, she couldn't imagine letting Cash go back to the rodeo without at least trying to work something out between them.

Besides, he had his daughter to think of now.

His daughter.

This kiss.

And that changed everything.

Didn't it?

She closed her eyes, savoring every second of togetherness.

Cash sighed, then put his hands on her shoulders and firmly pushed her away.

Her eyes snapped open.

He was staring down at her as if she'd suddenly developed leprosy.

He backed up, holding his hands palms out, as if he was mentally pushing her away as well as physically.

But why?

Had she done something wrong?

"Cash—what—" she croaked through a dry throat.

He was shaking his head frantically.

"No. No," he kept repeating.

"I don't understand."

"I'm sorry, Alyssa. This should never have happened. Forgive me. I—"

He couldn't finish his statement, but it didn't matter. She finished it in her own way.

He had just torn a hole in her heart.

Chapter Ten

What had he been thinking?

This couldn't be happening. This was a nightmare, only he wasn't dreaming.

And he would never be able to wake up, open his eyes and make everything right again.

His eyes were already open.

Wide-open.

His chest felt as if it were being plowed by a combine, the needle-sharp blades shredding his heart.

How could he have crossed the line, the one action that he'd promised himself he would never take, no matter how high his emotions ran?

He had kissed Alyssa.

And he had ruined everything.

He didn't even know how it had happened. He'd certainly not led her into a copse of trees at the park at twilight in order to take her into his arms and kiss her.

Far from it.

Rather, his intention had been to finally tell her the truth—the *whole* truth—about what had happened between him and Aaron on the night her brother died, even knowing she would never want to see or speak to him again.

She deserved to know what had really happened—and his role in it.

He couldn't keep this secret any longer. And it wasn't because Sharee had not so subtly threatened to tell the tale herself. Sharee had nothing to lose and possibly something to gain by blabbing everything, should they actually end up in court regarding custody of their daughter.

But it was his own conscience nudging him to be the man God was calling him to be. And that started with the truth.

And yet when he'd taken Alyssa's hands in his and she'd looked up at him, her expression so sensitive and sweet, empathy and concern radiating from her beautiful brown eyes, he'd lost his words.

More than that, he'd lost his mind.

Suddenly he'd wanted to kiss her more than anything in the world. That had been his last rational thought.

And when his mouth had touched hers, he was a goner.

The guilt he perpetually carried on his shoulders had taken too long to catch up with his heart and his actions, and now he'd made things oh so much worse.

Worse for him, yes, but he deserved every bit of the pain of heartbreak he was now experiencing and would continue experiencing indefinitely, because he'd known what he was doing—and he'd known better than to let himself become close to Alyssa, much less to act on his feelings.

He'd earned what was coming to him.

But his true concern was for Alyssa. He'd drawn her to him, kissed her, and she'd welcomed his embrace.

Now he was about to push her away.

Forever.

"Cash?" she questioned, her tone rich and husky. "What is it? What's wrong?"

He shook his head. "I didn't—I shouldn't have—"

She frowned. "You shouldn't have what? Kissed me?"

He wasn't good at reading people, but even he could see the pain of rejection molding her once soft expression into a set of hard lines and angles. He watched, despairing, as she struggled to surround herself with an emotional shield, so he couldn't hurt her any more.

He hesitated, giving her time to take a breath and prepare for what was to come. Not that anything she did would ever be enough.

But before he exploded the world as she knew it, he wanted her to know what this moment had meant to him—that the kiss they'd shared was the best thing that had ever happened to him.

That there was nothing more in the world he would like than to be able to pursue a genuine, long-term relationship with her—even if it was impossible.

"Answer me, Cash. Am I not good enough for you?"

"No. No—that's not it, at all. I wanted to kiss you, Alyssa. I've wanted to hold you in my arms for a long time now, and it's taken every bit of my willpower to keep myself away from you, from acting on my feelings."

"Why?"

He wasn't ready to answer that question yet.

"You're making it sound like I have some kind of contagious disease or something."

Any tender feelings they might have had left between them dissipated into the night air.

"I didn't mean for this to happen tonight, but I want you to know that I do care for you. More than you can possibly imagine."

"You're not acting like it. You are making less than no sense." Her raw voice sounded irritated, matching the frown that etched her brow.

"I know."

"If you care about me, then why are you balking?"

He tried to speak, but his throat felt like he'd swallowed a spoonful of gravel. He cleared his throat and gave it a second go.

"When I said earlier that I wanted to talk, it wasn't under false pretenses, in order to get you alone out here so I could kiss you."

"No?" He was surprised to find that she sounded disappointed by his admission.

"No. Although like I said, I'm not sorry that it happened. I just want you to know that I wasn't trying to take advantage of you before—well, before we talk."

"You weren't taking advantage of me. What we shared was mutual, and I'm not sorry it happened."

"No, but you will be."

"Stop talking in circles and just tell me what it is you think is so awful that I'm going to walk away from you. Because that's what you're worried about, isn't it?"

"Yes. I think you won't ever want to speak to me again. I *know* you won't."

"Why?"

There was that word again. Sticking like a knife.

"Are you drinking again, Cash? Is that what this is about? I know I once told you that was a deal breaker, but that was before I knew you. Now I understand how serious you are taking yourself in trying to clean up your life. If you've made a mistake and slipped up— well, we all do. You. Me. Everyone. All the time. That's why we need a Savior."

He needed a Savior, all right. Going to church the past few months had convinced him of that truth.

"It's about Aaron."

She looked confused for a moment, but then her face shone with relief. "Are you going to tell me that you used to argue over girls? Because Sharee let the cat out of the bag today?" She chuckled. "I'm not surprised, you know, although I thought you might have finally gotten past fistfights, being full-grown men. You two were always competing with each other, even back in high school."

"That was part of the reason we decided to compete in different events in rodeo," he admitted. "So we wouldn't always be at each other's throats."

"Surely it wasn't as serious as all that. Boys will be boys, right?"

"It started out that way. But that night ended up being the most terrible tragedy I could imagine."

He could tell the exact moment understanding dawned on Alyssa. Gasping, she took a step backward and brought a hand up to her throat.

"You're talking about the night Aaron died."

Suddenly he couldn't look at her, he was so ashamed. He crossed his arms and stared at the ground beneath his boots.

"Yeah."

"Tell me. Whatever it is, we can get through this together."

"No. I don't think so. Not this."

"Why?" she asked again, and he winced.

"Because Aaron is dead because of me."

He had stunned her into silence, and no wonder.

"I don't understand," she said at last. "Aaron died in a car accident, because he was driving while intoxicated and ran a red light. He was alone in the car."

"Yes, but he wouldn't have been driving at all that night if it wasn't for me."

Alyssa suddenly looked woozy, trembling and rocking on her feet. Cash reached for her elbow just as she sat down hard on the gravel path.

"Are you all right?" He crouched down next to her, brushing her hair back from her face and noticing the cold sheen of sweat on her brow.

She flinched away from him, and the movement tore at his chest.

He dropped down on his knees beside her, pressing his palms into the rough denim of his blue jeans. Thankfully, there wasn't any foot or bicycle traffic on the path right now to interrupt them.

Alyssa gave a little distressed hiccup. "You guys were fighting. That's what Sharee said. She was there?"

He scoffed softly, disgusted with himself.

"That's *why* we were fighting. Both of us wanted the same girl."

"Sharee," Alyssa murmured.

"Yes. Even though we had only met her that evening. She was throwing herself at both of us and encouraging us to duel over her. What started out as two arrogant roosters strutting their stuff and stroking their own egos ended up in a major fight.

"It wasn't the first time we'd ever fought over the

same girl, but our friendship was rock solid and always came before any buckle bunny. I don't know what was different, but for some reason that night things got out of hand and neither one of us backed off. Maybe because Sharee was stoking the fire. Maybe it was because we'd both had way too much to drink, or else we would have realized how stupid we were acting."

"A fistfight? As in you *punched* each other?"

"Not all of the face wounds found on Aaron came from the car accident. To be fair, I had a split lip and a black eye."

"That's the stupidest thing I've ever heard," she spat.

He nodded. He couldn't disagree with her. She was disgusted with him, but no more so than he was with himself.

"When it was clear that Sharee was going to go home with me, Aaron flipped out. Our competition had always been good-natured. Win some, lose some. And it had never come to exchanging blows. But that night, something was different. I've gone over and over it in my mind, and I just don't know."

He blew out a breath, lifted his hat and jammed his fingers through his hair, roughly combing the messy strands back from his forehead, not caring when his fingers caught in the tangles.

Alyssa didn't speak. She pulled her knees up to her chin and wrapped her arms around her legs. Not surprisingly, she wouldn't look at him anymore.

"I guess I was winning the fight, although to look at us both you probably wouldn't have been able to tell the difference. Before I knew what was happening, Aaron shoved me out of his way, grabbed his jean jacket from his chair and stalked off."

He squeezed his eyes closed and swallowed hard, the emotion burning like lava in his throat cutting off all his air.

"I should have gone after him, but I didn't."

Alyssa made a tiny squeaking noise. Cash desperately wanted to reach out to her but knew she would push him away.

"I didn't know he was going to get behind the wheel," he insisted. "If I had, I promise I would have made sure that never happened. But it didn't even occur to me that he was so wound up about our fight that he would drink and drive."

"So instead, you just went home with Sharee and left Aaron alone," she accused. "Some friend you turned out to be. You didn't even give him a second thought, did you?"

He groaned.

What else could he say? She was right.

It was enough of an answer to get Alyssa back on her feet, either purposefully or inadvertently kicking loose gravel into his face.

Whether she meant to or not didn't matter. He deserved it.

"You abandoned my brother." Her voice cracked as tears streamed from her eyes.

Cash's breath came in ragged gasps. It broke him to see her cry, and it was even worse knowing he was the one who had caused her tears.

He might not have been the one to put a drink into Aaron's hand or push him behind the wheel to drive, but he was still culpable for the death of his best friend.

He had killed Aaron.

And now, Alyssa knew it.

* * *

Alyssa gingerly stepped from one box to the next, using one palm against the inside wall of the shed to keep her balance. Some of the boxes had seen better days and her footing was precarious at best. She was thankful she'd decided to wear sneakers today and not the boots she usually wore.

One of these days she was going to organize this shed, replacing all the old cardboard boxes that now held Christmas ornaments and the like with plastic bins. It had been years since she'd given the shed a thorough cleaning and it had been on her to-do list forever.

But today was not that day.

Today, she had to pull all the Christmas decorations for the shop out from the back of the shed where they'd been stored since last Christmas and get everything set up in one day.

She hadn't meant to leave decorating the store to the last minute, but life had gotten the best out of her. Her emotions had slowed her down, pulling her into a mire she had trouble crawling out of, and despite her best efforts, it was all she'd been able to do just to finish arranging the cases and shelves for the Kickfire products that would soon be on display.

She'd probably be here until midnight at least, and then after Thanksgiving with her family, it would be an early, early Black Friday morning for her. The shops in Serendipity didn't do any of those ridiculous overnight specials the way big cities did, but it would take her a couple of hours at least, maybe more, to set up the front window Kickfire display.

There were at least a dozen boxes, and some of them

were heavy. Which was her own fault. Every year she added more and more embellishments to the Christmas theme. By the time the holiday had come and gone, she always felt the shop was too busy for her to spend time properly packing the ornaments. Instead, she threw everything into old boxes without giving any consideration to how she was organizing them.

Which meant she had a big mess to deal with when she pulled out the decorations the week before Black Friday. She usually didn't mind so much this time of year. Christmas was in the air and excitement bubbled over in her heart.

In her opinion, it was not possible to go overboard when preparing for her favorite time of the year. There was no such thing as too many Christmas decorations.

Except for the issue of hauling out all the boxes. And except that she'd waited too long to get started.

She sighed and brushed her hair out of her eyes with the back of her hand. Despite the moderate temperature outside, it was hot inside the shed and beads of sweat clung to her brow.

She wondered briefly if maybe she ought to cut back on decorations this year. With the way things were now, her life appeared to be on an unending downswing. This Christmas might very well be the worst one ever.

Her brother had recently passed away, her mom was MIA, her father was ill and now, thanks to Cash, she would once again be running Emerson's on her own during the busiest season of the year. Even worse, the renovations weren't quite finished, and a quarter of her store was still a mess of empty shelves and display cases where the Kickfire products were supposed to be. It would be all she could do to get all of the Kickfire products out on time. She'd wanted them to be couched in the best Christmas display ever. Now there wouldn't be a single twinkling light.

And forget having a *face* for the store. That ship had sailed right along with Cash's admission that he'd been fighting with Aaron the night her brother had died.

She wasn't certain she'd be able to find peace on Earth and goodwill toward men.

Not this year.

Especially when it came to *goodwill* toward one man in particular.

At the moment, she was feeling anything *but* goodwill toward Cash Coble. He had ruined her life in so many ways, she couldn't begin to count and didn't really want to. Like today, for example. The one day she really could have used Cash's muscle to help her and he was gone.

Permanently.

And good riddance to him.

Just thinking about him made her heart beat faster— and not in a good way. Fury flamed through her with sparks of betrayal painfully tailgating behind it.

She didn't need Cash. She didn't even want him here. Not in Serendipity, and most certainly not at Emerson's.

And she would keep telling herself that until she believed it. Because there was still a tiny niggle of doubt inside her heart telling her there might be more to the story than what he had admitted to.

Honestly, she didn't know what to think.

At first, she'd been so angry she'd been literally seeing red. If steam could have escaped from her ears, it would have. All she could see when she closed her eyes was Aaron, beaten both physically and emotionally, lurching behind the wheel of his car, his only thought to get away from the man he'd called his best friend.

But after she'd calmed down, she'd realized there was more to it than that. Cash had presented her with the truth as he saw it, from his perspective, and there was no doubt in her mind that he was carrying a heavy load of guilt on his shoulders.

But even as furious with him as she had been, she could still see how much Cash loved Aaron. It was right there in his eyes.

What had happened to Aaron wasn't a cut-and-dried story from anyone's lips. Rather, it was a convoluted mess, and it would take her time to sort out her thoughts and feelings.

But right now, she had a store to decorate.

By herself.

She sniffed her emotions away and mentally straightened her shoulders. It might take more effort on her part, but she was perfectly capable of doing this task on her own. She could do anything she put her mind to.

It wouldn't be the first time she'd had to carry large, heavy boxes by herself. Ever since her father got sick and Eddie had decided that riding a horse off into the distant sunset was more fun than fronting shelves and sweeping floors, Alyssa had been doing virtually everything in the store herself.

That is, until Cash had come barreling into her life

with his handsome face, strong arms and reliable work ethic. She couldn't deny, even to herself, that nothing, including going about her daily work, would ever be the same.

Cash had ruined everything.

She was beyond furious at how he'd weaseled his way into her life and how much she'd come to depend on him.

That was, perhaps, what hurt her the most.

All this time he'd been carrying around this big secret and he'd never even hinted at it. He'd had the audacity to let her believe he was her brother's best friend, and as if that wasn't duplicitous enough, she'd thought he was *her* friend. That he'd genuinely cared for her, as she did him—even when tender feelings had begun to bloom.

He'd even had the nerve to kiss her.

It might have started out innocently enough. There was no way he could have orchestrated the events that led them to spending time together originally.

After all, she had bid on him at the auction, not the other way around. He'd balked at the thought of working with her when he'd first started. But later on, after they'd become reacquainted, she couldn't help but think that he had purposefully engaged her feelings.

Toyed with her.

Betrayed her.

And she'd been betrayed one too many times in her life to let this time slide.

She huffed loudly. She needed to get out of her own head and get this job done instead of balancing precariously in the middle of a project, both literally and metaphorically, ruminating over things she had no control over.

She shifted forward to grab the next box from the pile. Directly in front of her, a stack of four old Christmas boxes rocked unstably. She yelped as the top box tipped over, falling straight toward her.

With a growl of dismay, she punched back at it, her fist going clean through the weakened cardboard and slicing into her wrist with the jagged edges formed by the hole made by her hand.

She cried out in surprise. She could already see rivulets of deep red blood forming on her skin.

The odd thing was, she knew this should hurt. Paper cuts were bad enough, but cardboard paper cuts were the worst.

And yet she felt nothing as the box rapidly became saturated with her blood. Apparently, the inward pain she was toiling with mentally overrode anything she might encounter physically.

Groaning, she pressed her other hand to the side of the box for support and removed her injured fist, the cardboard scraping against her already scratched skin and deepening the wound.

It might not hurt yet, but it was going to. She didn't relish the thought.

Great.

Now she was going to have to climb out of the shed and go clean out the wound and bandage herself up before she would be able to finish this not-so-fun part of this project. It was hard to tell how badly she'd been hurt because of all the blood covering her skin.

Hopefully there weren't any cuts deep enough to require stitches. If that happened, she'd lose the whole afternoon taking an unexpected excursion to see Dr. Delia.

With an irritated sigh, she cradled her bloody hand against her pastel-blue sweatshirt—which would no doubt have to be tossed in the Dumpster now that it was stained a dark crimson—and turned to pick her way back out of the shed.

She'd almost made it to the door when she stepped on a box filled with old papers that needed to be burned—yet another project Alyssa never had time to get to. The top flap was open because the box was overloaded and papers stuck out at random angles.

Her sneaker hit dead center on a stack of flyers and the sheets slipped out from underneath her, soaring every which direction. She immediately lost her balance and fell backward, spiraling her arms in an attempt to regain her equilibrium.

Stepping back with her other foot onto a different box, she pushed herself forward, hoping she could use the momentum to clear the rest of the cartons and jump out of the shed. Even if she didn't land on her feet, skinned knees would beat the potential of smacking the back of her head on something hard if she continued her backward fall.

The move worked, and she catapulted out of the shed headfirst. She instantly realized there was no way she would be able to land on her feet at this angle. The best she could hope for was to protect her head with her arms and tuck and roll.

Maybe falling backward would have been the better choice.

She wrapped one arm around her neck and reached

out with the already injured one to try to catch the brunt of her fall, but instead of her palm meeting gravel, it was wrapped in a large, steady hand, pulling her up and changing her trajectory as a strong arm wrapped around her waist, stabilizing her.

Instead of falling to the earth in an inglorious heap, she was able to regain her balance and land on her feet.

And end up held tightly in a man's embrace.

She didn't have to look up to know who had just rescued her.

"Cash," she whispered through a dry throat.

He was the last person on Earth she expected to see today, much less to be in exactly the right place at the right time to save her from what was sure to have been a painful fall.

He dropped her hand but continued to hold her around the waist, steadying her. She hoped he couldn't feel her quivering, a byproduct of the adrenaline coursing through her and not because of her proximity to him.

"You're bleeding," he exclaimed.

She would have been bleeding head to toe, had he not caught her.

He lifted her left hand, turning it over and carefully examining her wrist, his face set in a grim frown.

She'd been so shaken by almost taking a serious nosedive, she'd completely forgotten about punching the box.

She glanced down and surveyed the damage. Her wrist still didn't hurt, but there was a lot of blood. It was impossible to gauge how deep the cuts were until she washed the wound.

"Let's get you into the shop," he murmured.

She jerked her hand away. "It's no big deal."

"Maybe. Maybe not. But I'm not leaving until I know for sure I don't need to call Dr. Delia."

She ignored him as she paced back to the shop and let herself in the back door. She had too much to do today to deal with injuries, and way too much to do to deal with Cash. Her mind was racing as fast as her heart.

"What are you doing here?" Her voice was terse, and he pressed his lips into a hard, straight line.

"Just here to pick up my final paycheck. I won't be sticking around, so you don't have to worry about running into me on the street or in church."

She'd expected to feel relieved by his words. Seeing him was its own form of torture. And yet, the thought of never seeing him again caused an equal amount of agony.

"You don't have to leave because of me."

He stared at her for a long moment.

"Yeah, I think I do. But not until I'm sure your wrist is okay. You've got bad cuts and your sweatshirt is covered in blood."

She scoffed, ignoring him as she grabbed a washcloth and her first aid kit from a shelf in the back room and then moved to the sink to rinse off her hand with cool water.

She didn't need Cash here to help her.

It just figured that *now* it stung, and she winced despite her best intentions not to. And, of course, Cash saw her flinch as the cold water bathed her wound.

"Give me the washcloth," he murmured, taking the cloth and rinsing the blood out of it. With surprising tenderness, he held her hand and gently dabbed at the cuts on her wrist.

"How did this happen?" he asked, his gaze still on the cuts he was wiping clean.

"I punched a box."

"You did what? Why?"

I was thinking about you.

"To keep it from falling on top of me."

"What were you doing in the shed?"

"Pulling out the Christmas decorations. I am way behind where I need to be in order to have the Kickfire collection ready by this Friday."

"Why are you doing this alone?" he asked, and then faltered. "Oh. Oh, yeah."

"Yeah. That would be why."

"I'm sorry," he said, and Alyssa could tell he meant more than just that he hadn't been here to help her with the boxes today.

But words simply weren't enough. Not for Alyssa. Not yet.

"Some of these cuts are pretty deep," he said in an obvious attempt to change the subject.

"Not really." She pulled a roll of gauze and some antibiotic cream from the first aid kit. The cuts on her heart were much deeper than those on her wrist.

It would help if Cash would wrap her wrist for her. Doing it herself one-handed was a hassle. But he was busy fishing his cell phone from his back pocket.

"I think we ought to call Dr. Delia just to be on the safe side. You don't want them to get infected. I can take you down to her office now."

"I *don't* need a doctor," she insisted. "You are *totally* overreacting."

She spread the antiseptic cream over her wounds and started wrapping the gauze around her wrist. Hopefully that would prove to Cash that she didn't need a doctor's care.

He was still holding his phone in his hand, looking uncertain, when it rang.

His gaze widened when he read the caller ID, and then he frowned, his brow furrowing. He cleared his throat before answering.

"Sharee? What's up?"

There was a high, shrill chatter on the other end of the line. Alyssa could hear the voice but couldn't make out the words.

"Slow down," Cash said, his breath coming in short gasps. "Where are you?"

Sharee said something and Cash nodded.

"Do you have someone to take you to the hospital?"

Alyssa's ears perked up at the news.

"There's no reason to panic," Cash said. "Just do your breathing exercises or whatever and get to the hospital as soon as possible. I'll meet you there."

When he punched the end button, he pressed the phone to his chest and stared out the window, unseeing.

Alyssa tied off the gauze and moved to Cash's side, tentatively touching his bicep.

"Cash?"

"Sharee is in labor." His voice was deep and rich with emotion.

Their gazes met. She could see sparks of pure panic along with elation and his muscles quivered beneath her touch. She could only imagine how fast his pulse was hammering. Her own was thumping wildly and her nerves buzzed like a hive of bees.

"What hospital?" she asked, trying to get him to focus.

"St. Anthony's. Her mom is taking her. She—she wants me to be there." He choked on his words. "My daughter is coming into the world today."

"Would you like me to go with you?"

Chapter Eleven

Cash couldn't believe Alyssa had offered her support when she was so clearly—and rightly—still angry with him.

That wasn't something that would change with time. He knew there was no way to change things, no way to fix it.

And yet here they were, in the hospital elevator on their way to the fifth-floor maternity ward, side by side.

He'd been too nervous to talk much on their way to Dallas, and he didn't know what to say, anyway, so they'd ridden in an uneasy silence. Alyssa just stared out the passenger side window, lost in her own thoughts.

She'd taken the lead when they'd reached the hospital, asking at the information desk where the maternity ward was and where the elevator was located.

"You'll need to call Sharee when we reach the floor and let her know we're here."

Cash was already fishing his cell phone out of his pocket. The lady at the front desk had informed them that the hospital gave each mother a special door code they would only share with people they trusted and wanted to see.

He wasn't certain Sharee trusted him, and he didn't think he would be someone she'd want to see, either, especially now. But then again, she'd called him, and she'd sounded anxious for him to meet her at the hospital.

Not nearly as anxious as he was to be here. His baby daughter was about to be born. He was a bundle of nerves. He hoped he wouldn't quiver too much the first time he held his precious infant in his arms.

Taking a deep breath, he punched in the code and slid a glance at Alyssa when the lock turned green, allowing him to open the door.

"Why do you think she called me?" he whispered as they made their way down the hallway toward Sharee's room.

"Because you're the baby's father," she said, tucking her hand under his arm.

He didn't know why her touch reassured him as much as it did, but he would take it.

"Other than that, I can't say," she continued. "But don't worry about that right now. Just enjoy this moment and savor every second. You'll only get to experience the birth of your first child once."

His throat closed so tightly he couldn't breathe. He made a croaking sound and Alyssa chuckled.

"I think that pretty much sums up how every new father feels."

"Here we are," Alyssa said as they approached Sharee's room. "I can wait in the family room if you want."

He made a choking noise again and clutched her hand so tightly she winced. He loosened his grip and glanced at her hand. At least it was her right hand and not her injured left hand. In his current state, it was a mistake he could easily have made.

"Don't leave my side," he whispered, his voice husky. "Please."

"I'm right here," she assured him, putting her other hand over his.

The door was open, but Cash knocked on the jamb to announce their presence.

Sharee was half sitting in bed, her gaze fixed on the television, which was playing a soap opera. She glanced their direction but then returned her attention to the television, holding up one finger asking them to wait.

Sharee didn't appear to be in any distress. He waited, thinking she was between contractions, but even after five minutes, nothing changed, other than the soap opera going to a commercial.

"Finally," Sharee said, as if Cash hadn't rushed to her side as quickly as possible. "I wasn't sure you were going to come."

"You think I wouldn't want to be here for the birth of my daughter?" He couldn't help the bitterness that crept into his tone.

"No, you're right. I knew you'd come when I called you. Alyssa, you're welcome, as well."

"Where is your mother?" Alyssa asked.

Sharee made a dismissive gesture. "She's long gone. She dropped me at the door and drove off. Thankfully, nurses pay attention to a woman who is clearly in labor."

"Did your contractions stop after you got here?" he asked, perplexed.

Sharee laughed, but there was little mirth in the sound. "Oh, I've had plenty of contractions. I'm having one now, in fact. See the paper over there?" She pointed to a machine that was spitting out paper with scribbles on it that reminded Cash of a lie detector.

"The big rises and falls are contractions. You can see they are getting closer together."

Alyssa walked over to the machine, appearing fascinated by it. Cash thought it might be a way to give him and Sharee a modicum of privacy.

Cash was glad Alyssa was here with him. And he was frankly shocked that Sharee's mother wasn't here.

"Isn't your mom going to be your coach, or whatever it is?"

Sharee snorted. "As if. She doesn't even want to see the baby that makes her a grandmother."

Cash felt as if he'd been kicked in the gut. What kind of woman dropped her laboring daughter off at a hospital and left her there unattended?

"Well, I'm not leaving," he told her. "I will be here when my daughter is born."

"Which shouldn't be long now, if this machine is anything to go by," Alyssa said. "It looks like your contractions are getting really close together."

Sharee made a face. "Yeah. I hope it's soon. They won't let me eat and I'm starving. Laboring is hard work."

He shook his head in confusion.

"I had an epidural," Sharee explained. "I asked for one as they wheeled me up to the fifth floor. You know how demanding I can be when I want to be."

"So, you don't feel anything?"

"I can feel my muscles contracting, and there's lots of pressure, but no pain. I just want to get this over with."

Sharee *had* called him to be here, and he was about to ask what decision she'd made regarding their daughter, when she suddenly groaned.

"That was different," she said, her breath suddenly coming in short gasps.

"Should I get a nurse?" he asked.

"Please."

This was the most serious Cash had ever seen Sharee. She appeared to barely be aware of what was going on around her.

Cash rushed into the hallway and snagged the nearest nurse, telling her what had happened with Sharee.

Within minutes, the room was full of medical personnel. There was nothing he could do that wouldn't be getting in the way, so Cash moved to the far corner of the room and sat in the only chair, clasping his hands in his lap and whispering a prayer for Sharee and the baby.

To his surprise, Alyssa had moved to Sharee's side and was holding her hand and wiping her brow, murmuring encouragement to her.

Waiting was hard. Watching Sharee fight to bring their daughter into the world was even harder.

Unable to remain seated, Cash stood and looked out the window instead. He couldn't imagine how husbands watched their beloved wives giving birth.

If it was Alyssa on that bed—

But it wasn't Alyssa. It was Sharee. And they still hadn't worked out what was going to happen to the baby once she was born.

Suddenly the room, only moments before abuzz with voices and action, went completely silent.

What was wrong?

Cash whirled around, his heart in his throat. Everyone stood stock-still, staring at the tiny bundle in the doctor's arms. The doctor handed her off to a nearby nurse, who'd been ready and waiting with a receiving blanket.

The nurse gently but firmly rubbed the baby's chest as she smiled and cooed at her.

"Come on now, little girl, let's hear those lungs of yours."

For another moment, nothing happened. Cash's heart slammed against his chest. He wanted to do something, anything, to help his baby, but he was powerless.

"Lord, please," he whispered.

As if in answer to his prayer, the baby opened her tiny mouth and let out an enormous wail, clearly unhappy to have gone from the warmth of her mother's womb to the cold, bright world.

"There you go, love," the nurse said, placing the baby into Sharee's arms. "Get in some bonding time with Mama before we get you cleaned up and weighed."

Sharee's face blanched and Alyssa's distressed gaze met Cash's. Nothing had been decided, other than that Sharee did *not* want to bond with her infant.

"Take her and wrap her up," Sharee rasped through a dry throat. "Then give her to her father."

Cash reached for the chair and sat down hard.

Give her to her father.

Could that mean what it sounded like it meant?

Was he going to get to take his daughter home?

Alyssa's heart overflowed with joy at Sharee's words, and she gave the woman's shoulder a reassuring squeeze, but Sharee shrugged it away.

"It's no big deal," she mumbled wearily.

But it *was* a big deal. To Cash. To the baby. And to Sharee. Whatever Sharee's thoughts had been, and might still be, regarding the child-free life she wanted to live, she was doing something very brave here. Something strong.

"My lawyer already drew up the papers, Cash," Sharee said. "I'm giving you full custody. I've thought about it a lot. You've cleaned up your act, and you want our daughter. I can't say that right now. But when we talked, you gave me a lot to think about. I would— that is, I'd like you to send pictures of her to me from time to time."

"Of course," Cash agreed immediately, bounding out of his chair and approaching the bed. "Whatever you want. And I'll always leave it open for you to meet her."

"Your daughter is in good hands," Alyssa assured her. "Cash will be a great dad."

"You've made me so happy." Cash's voice was husky with emotion. "You have no idea."

Alyssa smiled at him. *She* knew what the gesture meant to him, and how relieved and full of joy he must be right now.

The nurse returned with the baby, now cleaned up and swaddled. She wasn't crying anymore but was sound asleep.

"A healthy six pounds, eight ounces and twenty-one inches," the nurse announced.

"Is that good?" Cash asked Alyssa.

"I think so," she responded.

"Dad, why don't you sit down on the chair over there

and hold your daughter," the nurse suggested, pressing the baby into his arms the moment he reached the chair.

For a long time, he just stared down at the little bundle of humanity sleeping in the crook of his arm.

"She's amazing," he whispered. He lifted his gaze to Sharee, but she wouldn't quite look at him. "What are we going to name her?"

Sharee shook her head. "That's for you and your girlfriend to decide."

"Oh, I'm not—" Alyssa started, but Cash cut her off.

"What do you think, Alyssa? Any names come to mind for the brightest star in my world?"

"Your star? You could call her Stella. That's Latin for *star.*"

"Baby Stella," Cash whispered. "It's perfect. Welcome."

A nurse returned with a bottle of formula and Cash fed Stella for the first time, not even complaining when more formula came back up and spread all over the shoulder of his black T-shirt than had stayed in her tiny tummy.

"There are certain tests we do before releasing Baby, so we'll keep her overnight," the nurse explained. "She's running just a bit of a fever. Nothing to worry about. But we are going to give her a round of antibiotics just to be on the safe side. You'll be able to take your little bundle of joy home with you tomorrow. I can bring in an extra chair for your girlfriend if you both want to stay. These chairs pull out to make beds—but I warn you they aren't very comfortable."

"Can you put them in a different room? I really need to get my beauty sleep," Sharee requested sharply.

The nurse agreed to the move, but Alyssa wasn't

sure what to do. Not surprisingly, Cash wasn't about to leave his daughter behind. And since he'd driven them both up to the hospital, that pretty much left Alyssa without options.

"You can drive my truck home and send someone back for us tomorrow," Cash suggested.

"I don't mind staying," she said, and laughed at the expression of utter relief that passed across Cash's face. He'd have baby duty all night and might need to be spelled from time to time.

If the nurse was surprised by Sharee's request, she didn't show it, and within an hour, Cash and Alyssa were ensconced in a small room in the far corner of the maternity ward. The room was a great deal smaller than the one Sharee had been in, but the privacy was nice. Cash offered her the bed while he took the chair and pulled Stella's bassinet up next to him.

He called his mother and let her know she was a grandma. Unlike Sharee's mom, Cash's mother was thrilled and immediately started making plans to fly down to Texas and spend some time with Cash and his new baby.

"I'll be taking her home on Thanksgiving Day. I can't think of anything more appropriate." He grinned.

Thanksgiving.

In all the excitement of Stella being born, Alyssa had put thoughts of the store and the family aside. She'd intended to get Emerson's ready to go today and then spend all of Thanksgiving with her father and Eddie.

"You and your mother—and Baby Stella, of course— are welcome to share our table at my dad's house for Thanksgiving dinner."

"Really?" She supposed it wasn't any big surprise

how stunned he looked, considering everything they'd been through.

She was shocked that she'd made the invitation.

She'd planned to share the cooking with Eddie, so she quickly phoned him and explained the circumstances. He assured her it wasn't a problem and he'd be happy to cook the entire holiday meal. He was just glad they'd all be together, and he was happy to hear Cash and his family would be joining.

Family get-togethers were more important to Alyssa than ever now that Aaron and her mother were gone. She hated that she might have to short shift her father and Eddie and sneak out to work on the store.

But maybe she was just putting too much pressure on herself. It wasn't perfect. Emerson's would be what it would be. She would do her best to get the displays up first thing on Black Friday.

Kickfire would just have to understand. Or not. The town, anxious to start their Christmas shopping, would likewise simply have to deal. How that would affect the store in the future was anyone's guess, but she had to do what she thought was right.

Cash wanted her here to help care for Baby Stella, and for tonight, they were her priority. Tomorrow— and the future—would take care of itself.

Chapter Twelve

Cash was surprised that Alyssa was willing to stay the night in the hospital to help him take care of Baby Stella.

He was scared to death at the thought of being left alone with the baby. Alyssa's presence was beyond reassuring. Plus, it removed any awkwardness he would otherwise have felt knowing Sharee was somewhere on the maternity ward.

He didn't know if Sharee would grieve over the choice she'd made, though he suspected she would. It would rip his heart out to be separated from Stella. But Sharee hadn't appeared to waver when she'd asked for Cash and Alyssa to be given another room. He prayed she'd find peace with her decision.

In the meantime, he was bonding with his precious daughter. He didn't know what he'd expected, but for this first night, at least, if he was wide-awake, it wasn't because Stella kept him up.

Alyssa had curled up on the bed and was dozing. She'd been under a lot of pressure and stress between renovating Emerson's for Kickfire and the stupid way he'd dropped the bomb about Aaron on her. She had needed to hear the truth, and hear it from him, but his timing could have been a lot better.

He should have waited until after her big Kickfire debut, so he could do his promo work for her and she could bask in her success.

As it was, he'd ruined everything. She was doing all her work alone. And now, by taking her away from the store just as she was about to put up her Christmas decorations and put the finishing touches on her Kickfire display, he'd made things even worse for her. Today, she might be thinking only of Stella, but Black Friday was going to come out swinging and she wouldn't be prepared.

What kind of woman made the kind of sacrifices Alyssa made? She was justly angry and feeling betrayed because of the way Cash had treated her, and yet when push came to shove, she hadn't given it a second's thought before stepping up to support him and Baby Stella.

Alyssa was one of a kind. She put her whole heart into everything she did, from caring for her family to keeping Emerson's Hardware afloat. She'd successfully courted the Kickfire brand.

And she'd opened her heart to him.

He hadn't realized just how much until they'd shared a kiss, but then, he hadn't realized the strength of his own feelings until then, either.

And now, watching his baby sleeping in her crib and Alyssa lightly snoring on the hospital bed, he finally knew what true love was.

This was what he wanted. Alyssa. Stella. A family to whom he could commit every bit of his love and protection. He hadn't done a good job of guarding Alyssa's heart, mainly because he'd been the one she needed defending from.

But none of that changed the fact that he was in love with her and wanted to spend his life with her.

He didn't know if she could ever really forgive him, but if anyone had the capability to find forgiveness in her heart, it was Alyssa.

He couldn't fix the past. But the more he thought about it, the more he started to think that maybe, just maybe, he might be able to change her future.

First thing in the morning, he had a couple of very important phone calls to make.

In the meantime, sweet Baby Stella had awoken and needed to be changed and fed. And as her daddy, it was now his privilege to care for all her needs.

The following morning, a lawyer visited and, as Sharee had promised, presented Cash with the necessary paperwork to give him full custody of Stella. He didn't even have to take a paternity test. Sharee wasn't fighting Cash at all.

Even so, Alyssa was relieved when the documents were signed and sealed, and a nurse came by with their release papers. The hospital provided Cash with a big bag of goodies to take home with him and Sharee had provided a car seat.

He still resided in a cabin at Howell's Bed and Breakfast, and his mother was on her way to meet her new granddaughter. But since Sharee hadn't given him any hint of what was to come, he wasn't prepared to bring a newborn home. And since it was Thanksgiving, no stores were open.

"I've got enough diapers and formula to last me a month," he said, "but where am I going to put this little one to sleep?"

"Let me stop by my friend Rachel's house. She runs an in-home day care and has a number of cribs and bassinets. I'm sure she can loan us something."

Cash kept expressing how grateful he was for her assistance, not just with the bassinet, but for coming with him to the hospital the day before and staying with him until he could bring Stella home.

She was happy to do it. She really was.

Watching Cash with Stella made it all worth it. She'd been so angry with him when he'd told her about Aaron, but after a while, she realized that most of those emotions came more from being piqued that he hadn't trusted her enough to tell her earlier, and not because what he'd done was unforgivable.

She'd seen him grow and mature in the past few months. She'd worked with him every day, watched him struggle with his alcoholism and come through it victorious, even during the worst times. She'd watched his strength of character as he tried to be the best person he could be for his daughter. And maybe best of all, she'd seen him return to the faith of his childhood and become a man of God.

And she loved him for it.

She loved *him*.

Her feelings had crept up on her and caught her by surprise, but once the words had gone through her mind and settled on her heart, she knew for certain.

She was in love with Cash, and with Baby Stella.

She'd once thought she might not ever have a family, especially after her own family imploded.

But now there was Cash and Stella and the possibility of something lasting.

She just didn't know how to express her feelings to Cash. Or when.

Right now, it was all he could do to be a daddy. She didn't want to overwhelm him by pressing him to make decisions that concerned her.

She wasn't even sure he still felt the same about her. They'd connected in an amazing way when they'd kissed, but much had happened since then.

Thanksgiving turned out to be a quiet, joyful time in the Emerson household. Her father was looking—and acting—especially well. Almost his old self. Alyssa didn't know what was responsible for the change, but she was happy for him.

Cash's mother, June, was a quiet, lovely woman who doted over Stella and engaged her father in conversation.

Eddie and Cash yapped on and on about his ranching work, and Alyssa realized for certain that he would never be back to help her run the store. Emerson's Hardware simply wasn't his path. She couldn't fault him for finding something he loved.

But that did leave her in a pickle. She would once again be working the store alone. And though she promised herself she wasn't going to worry about the Kickfire debut, she couldn't completely purge it from her mind as she, her brother and father, Cash and June played board games well into the evening while Stella was passed from lap to lap. Everyone wanted time with her, even Alyssa's dad. They shared a lot of talk and laughter, and she just couldn't find it in her heart to break away.

Her alarm rang at 3:00 a.m., way too early for any sane person to get up. But she hadn't even started decorating the store for Christmas, much less prepared the Kickfire display for its debut.

Cash had said the other day that he'd been ready to pick up his last check and leave. Hopefully that had changed now that he had Stella, but she didn't know if she'd see him today or not, what with the Kickfire publicity.

By the time she'd showered, blow-dried her hair and put on a little makeup, a half hour had passed. She must be nuts to be trying to save Black Friday from utter failure.

Still half-asleep, she decided to walk to the store, hoping the crisp early morning air would help get her brain cells moving. Once Cup O' Jo's opened at nine, she'd get a large cup of coffee, but in the meantime, she had a ton of work to do.

As she approached the store, she was surprised to find the light on. Had she left the light on when she'd rushed off with Cash?

But wait. That wasn't just the store light blaring out onto the dark street. It was soft, blinking colored lights—*Christmas* lights—in the window.

She peered into the window display, utterly stunned. Half was the large nativity scene, couched in hay, all the statues placed with care.

On the other side of the window, the shelf was covered with fluffy white cotton, and on top of that, a clever display of boots and hats. One male mannequin was dressed in Kickfire's best white chambray shirt and blue jeans and the female mannequin sported an equally impressive Western outfit.

Whoever created the scene had posed the mannequins so it appeared as if the female was throwing a snowball at the male and he was ducking so he wouldn't get hit. Serendipity rarely got snow, but the display was a work of art, and tears of gratitude flowed down Alyssa's cheeks.

She had no idea who did this for her, never mind when or how.

How did they even get into the store? She distinctly remembered locking the door behind her when she and Cash had taken off for the hospital.

And really, how had anyone known what she'd needed?

She let herself into the shop and simply marveled. Inside, the Kickfire display had been set and was ready to go. Decorations were already up and shining with Christmas spirit. There was a Christmas tree in the far corner. She merely had to put money in the register and she was ready to go for Black Friday.

She spent the next two hours making sure everything was stocked and fronted and that her store was looking the best it could, but the truth was, there wasn't much for her to do. The shop had been meticulously cleaned. There wasn't a speck of dust to be seen and the floor looked not only well swept, but mopped, as well.

At six, she heard keys in the lock and turned to find Cash letting himself in, Baby Stella asleep in the infant car seat.

He looked around and whistled.

"Wow. This is even better than I imagined."

"When we talked about the Kickfire debut, you mean?" she asked.

"Er—yeah, that."

She narrowed her gaze on him. "Why do I think there's more to this than you're telling me?"

He just grinned and shrugged.

At eight she turned the sign from Closed to Open, and customer after customer stopped by to see the new Kickfire products and express their excitement of having the new line sold in Serendipity. Fancy pranced around interacting with the customers, acting like the store mascot she was. The kittens had been adopted, all except Maus. Alyssa found it adorable that Cash had become so attached to the little black fur-ball.

Jo was one of the first to enter, and it didn't take much to get the whole story from her. Cash had called her and asked her to head up a committee to make sure Emerson's would be decorated and prepared for the Kickfire debut.

A little buzz around town and there were plenty of volunteers who offered to help.

"Many hands make light work," Jo told her.

"Yes, but how did you get in?" she wondered aloud.

Jo smiled widely. "Your father stopped by to do the honors."

"My *father*?" Alyssa didn't know whether to be excited or alarmed by the news that he'd come to the shop.

"It'll be a slow process, but I think he wants to come back to work, at least part-time."

"That's wonderful," she exclaimed.

Considering she thought the end of the world was coming this morning, things had certainly turned around. Now, if she could just find Cash and get her personal life in order, everything would be perfect. She glanced around the store, but apparently he'd slipped out when she hadn't been looking.

"He's already left town, love," Jo told her, guessing her thoughts as she glanced around.

"I guess he isn't going to be the face of Emerson's and Kickfire," she said, discouragement obvious in her tone.

"Oh, no. It's not that. Quite the opposite, in fact. He's visiting a television studio with Martin and Pete. He's going on the local news to show off all your fancy new duds and talk up Emerson's Hardware."

"Really?"

"I think there's going to be a big spread in *Rodeo Times* magazine, as well," she said. "Martin actually thinks this thing with Kickfire is just what Cash needs. If Martin has his way, Cash probably won't be returning to Serendipity in the near future. He'll be back on the pro rodeo circuit after this."

"Oh."

Alyssa's heart plunged into her stomach. Of course he would. That had been the plan all along. When it came time to cowboy up and be a daddy for Stella, he was right there. Now it was time for him to provide for her by doing what he knew—rodeo.

"Cash's mom will be watching Stella for at least the first couple of months while Cash works. From what I hear, she's thrilled to be a grandmother."

Alyssa forced a smile to her face. "I'm glad for her— for all of them. Stella is a precious little blessing."

Jo studied her for a long time before agreeing.

"It looks like Kickfire is a huge success," Jo added.

"With or without Cash sponsoring it. Although I'm sure that man's handsome face won't hurt."

Though she didn't say so, Alyssa privately disagreed. Today wasn't exactly a success. Everything would be different without Cash. Alyssa's heart would ache for his handsome face, his good heart and his sweet Stella for a good, long time.

Maybe always.

Chapter Thirteen

﹏

Alyssa had no idea why the church Christmas committee had chosen her to play Mary in the live nativity this year. There were much younger, much prettier young ladies who could do it.

But for some reason, they'd picked her—and they'd insisted on it. So on Christmas Eve, she dutifully donned the white dress and royal blue wrap and made her way to where the life-size crèche had been set up just outside the church.

The committee had gone all-out this year. There were several of Rowdy Masterson's sheep milling around, along with a donkey and a large tan dog that Alyssa guessed was supposed to be a camel. She'd never read any nativity accounts that had included dogs.

Several little boys were dressed as shepherds, while the little girls preferred angel costumes. Seth Howell's boy Caden even had a drum and was pounding out an uneven rhythm with his sticks.

Alyssa carefully seated herself on the hay bale behind the crèche, which she assumed had been placed there for her. People had started gathering for the service and everyone had an interest in what was going on in the live nativity scene, which in previous years had gone wild in any number of ways, from a young shepherd freaking out over the sheep he was supposed to be herding, to a particularly outgoing angel who thought she ought to have the sole speaking part.

Tonight, the only thing that appeared to be missing was a baby to play Jesus and, ironically enough, Joseph. It was bad enough that the town probably thought she couldn't catch a husband in real life without being stood up when she was playing the mother of God.

Alyssa was grateful when Jo rushed up with a baby in her arms. Traditionally, the role of Jesus went to the newest baby in town, but Alyssa didn't know of any, at least not newborn, as the baby placed in her arms clearly was.

She glanced down and took a good look at the baby.

It couldn't be.

But there was no doubt. Even if her eyes didn't show her the truth, her heart confirmed it.

She was holding Stella in her arms.

And that meant—

"Sorry I'm late. I had some trouble with my costume." *Cash.*

He was back. But why?

"I didn't expect to see you here," she admitted.

"No? But I thought it was traditional for Serendipity's newest resident to play the role of Jesus."

Newest resident?

"It is, but—you'd have to live here for her to be considered a resident."

"Exactly. The Howells have kept my cabin for me for the time being, and as you know, my mom is staying with me for a couple of months—just until I get my bearings as a father. But I'm hoping to be looking for a family home soon."

Alyssa didn't even know what to say to that, and she wasn't even sure she could speak if she tried.

"If there's one thing I've learned through Aaron's death, it's to treasure each day that God gives us. Each moment is so precious. That's why I'm here. To ask your forgiveness."

"Done." Alyssa didn't even have to think about it. "Life is too short to hold a grudge. Besides, when you remain angry with someone, it only hurts you, not the person you're mad at."

"You are an amazing woman, you know that?"

She flashed him a wry grin. "Is it the costume?"

"Well, Mary was an amazing woman, too, but I'm talking about you."

Alyssa's heart swelled until she thought it might burst. "You are perfect for Joseph. Strong and protective."

He stepped one foot onto the hay bale and leaned on his cane. "It's the shepherd's hook, right?"

She laughed. "It's a bit more than that."

"Speaking of costumes, I think you forgot something. Yours doesn't look quite right."

"It—what did I forget?" she stammered.

"Hang on." He yanked up his robe until he could reach the front pocket of the jeans he was wearing underneath. He dug around for a moment and then grinned as he held out a diamond ring between his thumb and forefinger. "Here we go. I specifically remember in the story that Mary was engaged to a man named Joseph. So, what do you say?"

She wasn't certain she could say anything. Her throat closed around her words. But finally, she managed a chuckle. She pressed a kiss to Stella's forehead and laid her on the soft hay in the manger.

"That depends. Am I speaking as Mary or as myself?"

His gaze widened. "Will it make a difference in your answer? I don't mind saying I was kind of hoping not."

"Well, let's see. Mary said yes to Joseph, right?"

He groaned. "You're killing me here."

Stella gurgled and wriggled in her swaddling blanket.

"Now see? You've got Stella all antsy, too. So, tell us, Alyssa Joan Emerson. Will you marry me and make us a real family?"

"But what about rodeo?"

He shook his head. "What about rodeo?"

"I thought you were going back. I heard Martin was pleased with the Kickfire shoot."

"Yeah, for about five seconds, until I told him I was only doing it for you and had no intention of returning to rodeo. Which reminds me. I know your dad is talking about coming back to work part-time, but I was wondering if I might get an application for employment. I'm looking for something long-term and stable. You know, something that a married man with a family would do?"

She pressed her palm to his chest and felt his heart thumping wildly.

"These last few weeks have been awful for me. I didn't know where you went after your Kickfire shoot. I assumed it was back to rodeo. I tried to tell myself that it didn't matter, but it does matter. Because I love you, and I love Stella, and I can't imagine my life without you two in it."

"So, just to clarify, that's a yes, then? From you, and not just the character you're playing?"

"Absolutely, positively, one hundred percent yes."

With that, she threw herself into his arms and kissed him the way she'd wanted to kiss him since the moment she realized she was in love with him.

"Um, excuse me," came Jo's voice from somewhere in the distance.

Heat rushed to Alyssa's face as she realized they had an audience—a big audience.

"That's by far the most unusual version of the nativity I've ever had the privilege of seeing," Jo said with a throaty cackle, "but I think I can safely say God is looking down and smiling on you two. No— make that *three*."

The churchgoers around them broke into applause. Alyssa's blush flamed even hotter, but Cash just took her hand and bowed as if he was taking a curtain call.

"Thank you very much. If you would like to use us in future theater productions, you can find us at our family store, Emerson's Hardware."

That appeared to appease the crowd, and in another couple of minutes, they were left alone.

"We need to go change out of our costumes and get ready for the midnight service," Alyssa reminded him.

"Right. Oh, and did I tell you I got a sponsor? I went to my first AA meeting the other night, now that I don't have to worry about my public image. Frank Spencer took me on, if you can believe it. If anyone can keep me on the straight and narrow, it's Frank."

"I didn't even know he was an alcoholic."

"I think that's how he likes it. But he's stepped up for me in a big way."

"That's wonderful."

"Yes. But not as wonderful as you agreeing to be my wife. Say it again, just for me."

"I said it just for you the first time."

"Yes, I know, but we had an audience. Humor me."

Stella wailed, and Cash picked her up, cradling her in his arm. "I guess we still have a small audience."

Alyssa chuckled and placed her palms on his scruffy cheeks, holding his gaze with hers.

"Cash Coble, there is nothing in the world I'd like more than to marry you, to be your wife and Stella's mama."

"Now, that's more like it, sweetheart. Come here and kiss me, the Future Mrs. Coble. We have a lot of living to do."

* * * * *

Dear Reader,

What fun it is to head back into Serendipity, Texas and auction off yet another bachelor for the town's First Annual Bachelors and Baskets Auction benefiting the senior center.

It's amazing how one second can change everything. For Cash Coble, the death of his best friend Aaron imploded his world. For Alyssa Emerson, her dear brother Aaron's death broke apart her family. It's only when the two of them connect and support each other that they learn to move forward.

No matter what the situation, the one cornerstone we can always count on is Jesus. He never moves but is right beside us all the way. Sometimes it's harder to see and feel Him there with us, but the Bible assures us we can always count on His divine love and mercy.

I'm always delighted to hear from you, dear readers, and I love to connect socially. You can find my website at www.debkastnerbooks.com, where I hope you'll join my mailing list to learn of new projects and special offers. Come join me on Facebook at Debkastnerbooks, and you can catch me on Twitter @debkastner.

Please know that I pray for each and every one of you daily.

Love courageously,
Deb

Get 4 FREE REWARDS!

We'll send you 2 FREE Books plus 2 FREE Mystery Gifts.

Love Inspired® books feature contemporary inspirational romances with Christian characters facing the challenges of life and love.

FREE Value Over $20

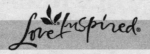
Rainbow Girl stepped into his field of vision from the kitchen area. *"Hallo."*

Eli's insides did funny things at the sight of her.

"Did you need something?"

He cleared his throat. "I came for a drink of water."

"Come on in." She pulled a glass out of the cupboard, filled it at the sink and handed it to him.

"Danki."

She gifted him with a smile. *"Bitte.* How's it going out there?"

He smiled back. "Fine." He gulped half the glass, then slowed down to sips. No sense rushing.

After a minute, she folded her arms. "Go ahead. Ask your question."

"What?"

"You obviously want to ask me something. What is it? Why do I color my hair all different colors? Why do I dress like this? Why did I leave? What is it?"

She posed all *gut* questions, but not the one he needed an answer to. A question that was no business of his to ask.

"Go ahead. Ask. I don't mind." Very un-Amish, but she'd offered. *Ne,* insisted.

He cleared his throat. "Are you going to stay?"

She stared for a moment, then looked away. Obviously not the question she'd expected, nor one she wanted to answer.

He'd made her uncomfortable. He never should have asked. What if she said *ne*? Did he want her to say *ja*? "You don't have to tell me." He didn't want to know anymore.

She pinned him with her steady brown gaze. "I don't know. I don't want to, but I'm sort of in a bind at the moment."

Maybe for the reason she'd been so sad the other day, which had made him feel sympathy for her.

He appreciated her honesty. "Then why does our bishop think you are?"

"He's hoping I do."

His heart tightened. "Why are you giving him false hope?" Why was she giving Eli false hope?

"I'm not. I've told him this is temporary. He won't listen. Maybe you could convince him to stop this foolishness—" she waved her hand toward where the building activity was going on "—before it's too late."

He chuckled. "You don't tell the bishop what to do. *He* tells you."

He really should head back outside to help the others. Instead, he filled his glass again and leaned against the counter. He studied her over the rim of his glass. Did he want Rainbow Girl to stay? She'd certainly turned things upside down around here. Turned him upside down. Instead of working in his forge—where he most enjoyed spending time—he was here, and gladly so. He preferred working with iron rather than wood, but today, carpentry strangely held more appeal.

Time to get back to work. He guzzled the rest of his water and set the glass in the sink. *"Danki."* As he turned to leave, something on the table caught his attention. The door knocker he'd made years ago for Dorcas—Rainbow Girl—ne, Dorcas, but now Rainbow Girl had it. They were the same person, but not the same. He crossed to the table and picked up his handiwork. "You kept this?"

She came up next to him. *"Ja.* I liked having a reminder of…"

"Of what?" Dare he hope him?

She stared at him. "Of…my life growing up here."

That was probably a better answer. He didn't need to be thinking of her as anything more than a lost *Englisher*.

Don't miss Courting Her Prodigal Heart *by Mary Davis, available January 2019 wherever*
Love Inspired® *books and ebooks are sold.*

www.LoveInspired.com

Looking for inspiration in tales
of hope, faith and heartfelt romance?

Check out **Love Inspired**® and
Love Inspired® **Suspense** books!

New books available every month!

CONNECT WITH US AT:

Facebook.com/groups/HarlequinConnection

Facebook.com/HarlequinBooks

Twitter.com/HarlequinBooks

Instagram.com/HarlequinBooks

Pinterest.com/HarlequinBooks

ReaderService.com

Time was running out for Celeste Alexander. Her fingers
flew over the keyboard, knowing each keystroke could be
her last before US marshal Jonathan Mast arrived to escort
her to her new life in the witness protection program.

"You gave her a laptop?" US marshal Stacy Preston
demanded. "Please tell me you didn't let her go online."

"Of course not! She had a basic tablet, with the internet
capability disabled." US marshal Karl Adams shot back
even before Stacy had finished her sentence.

The battery died. She groaned. Well, that was that.

"You guys mind if I go upstairs and get my charging
cable?"

The room went black. Then she heard the distant sound of gunfire erupting outside.

"Get Celeste away from the windows!" Karl shouted. "I'll cover the front."

What was happening? She felt Stacy's strong hand on her arm pulling her out of her chair.

"Come on!" Stacy shouted. "We have to hurry—"

Her voice was swallowed up in the sound of an explosion, expanding and roaring around them, shattering the windows, tossing Celeste backward and engulfing the living room in smoke. Celeste hit the floor, rolled and hit a door frame. She crawled through it, trying to get away from the smoke billowing behind her.

Suddenly a strong hand grabbed her out of the darkness, taking her by the arm and pulling her up to her feet so sharply she stumbled backward into a small room. The door closed behind them. She opened her mouth to scream, but a second hand clamped over her mouth. A flashlight flickered on and she looked up through the smoky haze, past worn blue jeans and a leather jacket, to see the strong lines of a firm jaw trimmed with a black beard, a straight nose and serious eyes staring into hers.

"Celeste Alexander?" He flashed a badge. "I'm Marshal Jonathan Mast. Stay close. I'll keep you safe."

Don't miss
Amish Hideout *by Maggie K. Black,*
available January 2019 wherever
Love Inspired® Suspense books and ebooks are sold.

www.LoveInspired.com

LISEXP1218

Inspirational Romance to
Warm Your Heart and Soul

Join our social communities to connect
with other readers who share your love!

Sign up for the Love Inspired newsletter
at **www.LoveInspired.com** to be the
first to find out about upcoming titles,
special promotions and exclusive content.

CONNECT WITH US AT:

Facebook.com/groups/HarlequinConnection

 Facebook.com/LoveInspiredBooks

 Twitter.com/LoveInspiredBks

LISOCIAL2018